"This is why I didn't want children. But we're h.... so we'll do wh.... marry me."

"No…" Cinnia said .... her lips white.

Henri drew in a tested breath, frustration returning in a flood of heat. "Did you hear what I just said?"

"Yes, I heard you. Fine. I'll live behind your iron curtain, but—" She swallowed. "But I won't marry you."

Her chin came up in what he knew was her standing-her-ground face. His ears buzzed as he sifted through her words. "What do you mean?"

"I mean I'll live with you, but I won't *live* with you." She flushed and pulled her shoulders up defensively around her ears.

"You don't want to sleep with me?" His heart bottomed out. She couldn't mean that.

She flinched and looked away, blinking hard. "No. I don't."

"Liar." It came out of him as a breath of absolute truth.

The Sauveterre Siblings

Meet the world's most renowned family…

Angelique, Henri, Ramon and Trella—two sets of twins born to a wealthy French tycoon and his Spanish aristocrat wife. Fame, notoriety and an excess of bodyguards is the price of being part of their illustrious dynasty. And wherever the Sauveterre twins go, scandal is sure to follow!

They're protected by the best security money can buy—no one can break through their barriers… But what happens when each of these Sauveterre siblings meets the one person who can breach their heart…?

Meet the heirs to the Sauveterre fortune in Dani Collins's fabulous new quartet:

Pursued by the Desert Prince
March 2017

His Mistress with Two Secrets
April 2017

Ramon and Isadora's story
Coming soon!

Trella and Prince Xavier's story
Coming soon!

HIS MISTRESS WITH TWO SECRETS

BY
DANI COLLINS

First Published in Great Britain 2017
By Mills & Boon, an imprint of HarperCollins*Publishers*
1 London Bridge Street, London, SE1 9GF

© 2017 Dani Collins

ISBN: 978-0-263-92419-0

Our policy is to use papers that are natural, renewable and recyclable
products and made from wood grown in sustainable forests. The logging
and manufacturing processes conform to the legal environmental
regulations of the country of origin.

Printed and bound in Spain
by CPI, Barcelona

Canadian **Dani Collins** knew in high school that she wanted to write romance for a living. Twenty-five years later—after marrying her high school sweetheart, having two kids with him, working at several generic office jobs and submitting countless manuscripts—she got 'The Call'. Her first Mills & Boon novel won the Reviewers' Choice Award for Best First in Series from *RT Book Reviews*. She now works in her own office, writing romance.

Books by Dani Collins

Mills & Boon Modern Romance

The Secret Beneath the Veil
Bought by Her Italian Boss
Vows of Revenge
Seduced into the Greek's World
The Russian's Acquisition
An Heir to Bind Them
A Debt Paid in Passion
More than a Convenient Marriage?
No Longer Forbidden?

The Sauveterre Siblings

Pursued by the Desert Prince

The Wrong Heirs

The Marriage He Must Keep
The Consequence He Must Claim

Seven Sexy Sins

The Sheikh's Sinful Seduction

The 21st Century Gentleman's Club

The Ultimate Seduction

One Night With Consequences

Proof of Their Sin

Visit the Author Profile page
at millsandboon.co.uk for more titles.

Dear Reader,

Henri is the oldest of the Sauveterre twins. After his sister was kidnapped he decided never to marry and have children, fearing they would become targets. He doesn't resent being a twin, but he knows who he is beyond that label. He's very singular…likes control and routine. Life is unpredictable enough without improvising your way through it—that's his attitude.

Cinnia is also very practical, and independent to a fault. As far as mistresses go, she was the perfect match for Henri, demanding little from him. That was why he was so blindsided when she left him.

I adore it when this happens to our alpha males—when they are über-confident and think they have their lives well in hand and then…*wham!* The heroine straightens her spine and slams the door behind her.

Cinnia is pregnant, and she knows exactly how Henri will react. *Badly!* But if they can make the jump from defensive and aloof to realizing they are perfect for one another, they have a chance at real happiness. I'll let you turn the page and discover for yourself how they make out.

Enjoy!

Dani

Dedication

For my parents,
who are celebrating their 50th wedding anniversary
as I write this. Much love always from #1.

PROLOGUE

As SHE ENTERED the clinic from the stairwell, Cinnia Whitley almost knocked the door into a woman standing inside. Cinnia murmured a distracted apology, thinking she might have seen her before, but not here. She would remember someone so tall and stiff and alert standing in that particular place.

Wait. Was she a guard? It was an odd place to hover. Maybe that's why she seemed so familiar. After spending two years with sober-faced watchmen dogging her movements, perhaps it wasn't the face she recognized so much as the attitude.

Because, if the woman was merely a relative waiting on a patient, there was a very comfortable lounge at the front of the clinic. The back entrance was for people like Cinnia, the paranoid ones who crept in through the building's underground car park in hopes of keeping her visit to this prenatal specialist strictly confidential.

Cinnia didn't bother speculating who the celebrity patient could be. She had bigger fish to fry. She was here for a scan to confirm suspicions on why she was expanding so quickly.

No, she kept thinking, absolutely refusing to entertain the most likely reason. She had a lot of work to get through in the next twenty-two weeks and had struggled to find time for another morning off for this test. If the doctor's suspicions were correct, her entire future would have to be recalibrated.

Twins? Really? *No.* Multiple births weren't even hereditary when they were identical and she thought only mothers passed along the fraternal trait. A father with an identical brother and two younger, identical twin sisters couldn't pass that to his offspring.

Could he?

Henri did whatever he wanted. She knew that much.

She did not miss that arrogance, or him, or the life he led with guards like that one dogging his every step, she assured herself with another flick of a glance at the woman by the door.

So why did she spend her mornings combing through online gossip pages, reading every scrap she could find about him? Reading that Henri was back to his old ways of dating and dropping was pure self-destruction, but at least there wasn't much written about that. His twin, Ramon, was stealing all the thunder, still racing and winning while doubling down with his own passionate exploits through a rotation of women who were loved and left.

The Sauveterres were a private lot, despite their domination of the media. But in her time with Henri, Cinnia had noticed that Ramon always seemed to make a splash in the papers when something was going on with the family, like he was deliberately pulling the attention.

Her breakup with Henri was two months ago. Old news by now. It must be Angelique he was trying to cover for.

The brothers were insanely protective of their younger sisters, which was understandable given Trella's kidnapping when she was a child. Angelique was the only one seen in public these days and was becoming quite notorious, what with her affair with the Prince of Zhamair—or rather both him *and* the Prince of Elazar, if the online rags were to be believed.

Cinnia frowned, still thinking there was something about the photo of Angelique with the Prince of Elazar that wasn't right. Impossibly, she had thought it was actually Trella in that photo, but Trella was a recluse. Cinnia had only met her in person a couple of times.

The nurse was on the phone and finally noticed her. Cinnia waved a greeting and tried to smile past her jumbled thoughts. Tried not to think of Henri and twins. It was too big and scary to absorb unless she was forced to.

The nurse indicated to a clerk that Cinnia was here. The clerk nodded and turned to the cabinet to pick out her file.

Cinnia loosened her scarf and started to unbutton her coat, pleased to be warm and dry when it was such a tremendously miserable day, even by London's late-February standards.

Behind her, a door to an exam room opened, startling her into stepping out of the way and turning.

"Oh. Excuse me," the woman said.

"My fault—" Cinnia began, then blurted, "Oh, my God!" as she recognized that model-like physique and those aristocratic features. "I was just thinking about you!"

"Cinnia!" Angelique beamed and they went in for a hug like long-lost sisters, affection squeezing Cinnia's arms tight around the other woman, her excitement completely overriding what should have been *way* more caution on her part.

The reality of Cinnia's situation hit belatedly and continued to strike in successive slaps over the next few seconds.

Cinnia felt Henri's sister stiffen as she came up against Cinnia's baby bump beneath the layers of her clothes.

Don't tell him, Cinnia thought with panic.

They drew back. Cinnia knew she wore a look of horror, which was awful when she was actually happy about the baby, happy to see—

"Oh, my *God*," Cinnia whispered. "I thought you were your sister."

Cinnia had always been able to tell the twins apart quite easily. It had been surprise and a quick glance and an even quicker assumption that had made her mistake Trella for Angelique. Trella never left the compound in Spain without one of her siblings accompanying her.

Did that mean Henri was here? Cinnia looked around with alarm, only seeing the guard.

Of course—that's why the guard seemed familiar. She'd seen her at Sus Brazos, the Sauveterre family home in Spain. This was Trella, even though there was nothing distinct to tell the women apart, Cinnia just knew by something in their demeanor. Angelique had that hint of reserve that Henri wore, while Trella had the radiance of warmth that Ramon projected.

Then it hit that not only was it odd for Trella to be out in public, with no family in sight, but *she was also in a prenatal clinic.*

"Oh. My. *God*."

What was the normally cloistered Sauveterre twin doing in London? Holding a bottle of prenatal vitamins and looking guilty as hell? How did a woman who lived like a nun and had female guards get herself pregnant? Henri was going to lose his mind!

Trella tucked the bottle behind her back and opened her mouth, but only a weak *um* came out.

Cinnia's eyes were widening to the point they stung. She was pretty sure they were going to fall right out of her head.

She watched Trella's gaze narrow as the full scope of

where they were and why penetrated her side. Cinnia's blood pressure had been stable so far, but her limbs began to tingle and her head went so hot she felt like her hair was on fire. She was pretty sure whatever breaths she was managing to draw lost all their oxygen before hitting her lungs.

"Are you…okay?" Cinnia asked hesitantly. She didn't know exactly what Trella had been through when she had been kidnapped, but she knew it had left her afraid of men for a long time. Afraid of a lot of things.

Trella, being an enormously resilient and self-deprecating person, let out a choke of hysterical laughter and rolled her eyes. It was a "look where I am," and her shrug conveyed that she was dealing with an unplanned pregnancy, but not one caused by something traumatic.

"How about you?" she challenged with wry cheer, then sobered. She frowned at Cinnia's middle. "Is it…?" She glanced around.

Henri's. That's what she was asking.

Cinnia's eyes teared up. *Please don't tell him*, she silently pleaded.

This was part sitcom, part Greek tragedy. Her own hysterical laugh pressed for escape, but her tight throat wouldn't release it.

Trella straightened her spine so she was that little bit taller than Cinnia. She gave her wavy dark hair a toss.

"We'll pretend this didn't happen." She was a stunning woman in her midtwenties, but she looked nine years old, hiding stolen candy and bravely pretending it wasn't in her red-hot hand.

This was the sister Henri had told Cinnia had existed in his childhood, the brat who had driven him crazy getting herself into trouble, always needing her big brother to step in and fix it.

Cinnia wanted to hug her again. She was so proud of

Trella, even if conquering her past had led to a complicated future.

And she desperately wanted to share this moment with Henri, instinctively knowing that after the shock, this sign of healing in Trella would be a much-needed bright spot.

Or not. Worrying about any Sauveterre would sit heavily on him. Taking care of his mother and sisters was as much responsibility as he was willing to shoulder. That's why he'd drawn such a hard line against marrying and procreating.

A wistful sigh filled her, but she held it in. Ironic that she wanted to be there for him as he dealt with his sister's news knowing full well he would lose his mind once he learned Cinnia was carrying *his* child.

I told you from the beginning I would never marry you.

Her heart clenched afresh, abraded and stung. *Scorned.*

"Ms. Whitley," the nurse said behind her. "I can take you now."

"It's really good to see you," Cinnia said to Trella, holding out her arms for another quick hug. "I've missed all of you."

Most of Cinnia's interactions with Henri's family had been over the tablet, but she felt the loss of connection to the Sauveterre clan quite deeply.

"I would ask you to give my regards to everyone, but…" Cinnia trailed off.

Trella's arms were firm and strong around her. She pulled away slowly, tilting her head so they were eye-to-eye. Would her baby have those Sauveterre eyes, Cinnia wondered with a pang? *Babies?*

"You and I can stay in touch now," Trella said with a conspiratorial twitch at the corners of her mouth. Her expression sobered to concern. "*Can* I call you? I'd like to know why…"

Cinnia knew that keeping the pregnancy from Henri was a losing battle. She just wanted a plan in place before he found out so he wouldn't feel trapped. Trella was far too close to her siblings to keep her own pregnancy a secret from them for long. Once she spilled those beans, Cinnia's condition would be quick to follow.

But if she could buy a little time to get her ducks in a row, maybe find out exactly how many babies she was actually having…

She nodded. "If you're still in London at the end of the week, why don't we have dinner?"

CHAPTER ONE

Two years ago...

CINNIA WAS NOT a social climber, but her roommate, Vera, was. Cheerfully and without apology. Thus, when Vera wangled opening-night tickets from the owner of *the* hottest new nightclub in London, she demanded Cinnia accompany her.

"I told him about your title," Vera said. "That's how I got him to say yes to our coming."

"The title that belongs to my great-uncle a million times removed whom I've never met and who wouldn't know me from Eve?"

"I might have exaggerated how close you are. But I told him about your granny's vintage tiara and since his theme is 'flappers and gangsters,' and he wants window dressing, he said we could come as staff. No swag," Vera said with a dismayed wrinkle of her nose. "Just mingle with the guests. Be first on the dance floor, that sort of thing."

Cinnia was reluctant. Her weekends were her only time away from her job at a wealth management firm to put the pieces in place for striking out on her own. She had set September as her goal and had a mile-long list of to-dos to make it happen.

"You work too hard," Vera groaned. "Look at it as a

chance to rub elbows with potential clients. This will be wall-to-wall, top-tier, A-list celebs."

"That's not how it works."

Cinnia's mother saw a different opportunity when Cinnia spoke to her over the tablet. "Tell me I can't wear the tiara so I can tell Vera there's no point."

"Nonsense. We'll get my dress out of storage, too. It's time they both saw some use. You, too, for that matter." Her mother had purposely held a Roaring Twenties party on her tenth anniversary so she could wear her grandmother's modest, heirloom tiara. She had had a beaded dress made special for the occasion.

"You wouldn't get the tiara from the safe-deposit box when we were broke and I wanted to sell it, but you'll let me wear it to a nightclub?" Cinnia asked, askance.

"This is why I kept it, for you girls to wear on special occasions. Go. Have fun. There's bound to be some nice men there."

"Rich husbands, you mean? They don't sell them at the bar, Mum."

"Of course not. It will be an open bar for something like this, won't it?" her mother returned tartly.

There was a reason she and her sisters called their mum Mrs. Bennet. She was forever trying to find their golden ticket of a husband. There was also a reason she was so determined to do so. The Whitleys had descended from aristocracy. The blue blood cells had been significantly diluted by bright, peasant red, but Milly Whitley was determined that her daughters *would* make good matches and the Whitleys *would* return to the lofty position they'd all enjoyed before Mr. Whitley had died and his fragile financial house of cards had toppled around them.

Until then, they would dress the part and hang on to a

house that was a money pit and they would attend the sorts of occasions that told the world they hadn't gone anywhere.

"I daresay you'll find a better class of suitor than your usual struggling students and apron clingers," her mother added snobbishly.

All they needed was one man with deep pockets.

Or, as Cinnia had said countless times, they could all get proper jobs like normal people.

Her two middle sisters decried that as blasphemy.

Priscilla, her first younger sister, was a *model*. Genuinely pretty, but not in high demand. Two years out of school and she had barely worked at all. She just needed a better head shot or a new outfit or a change of hairstyle and her career would take off, she kept assuring them. Completing a course in hairstyling or something useful like that would only hold her back.

Nell, their stunning little party girl, didn't need a job. Boys already bought her things and *she* was the one who would land them the Big Fish when the time came. If Cinnia could somehow keep her in school long enough to complete her A levels without getting pregnant, she'd be thrilled.

Thankfully Dorry had a brain and ten times anyone's ambition to use it. Their youngest sister had been babysitting from the moment she was old enough to wipe a nose and currently had a job in a fish-and-chip truck, much to their mother's repulsion. Dorry squirreled her money before anyone saw it and kept her head down, usually bent over a book. If something happened to Cinnia, she had every confidence her baby sister would keep the rest of them fed and sheltered.

She was trying not to put that on poor Dorry. After trying to help her mother win a fight against owing back taxes and other debts associated with her father's estate,

Cinnia had taken an interest in wills and estate planning. As careers went, it paid well enough, was stable and flexible and she found it intellectually challenging.

Her mother said she might as well be an undertaker.

Vera said, "No matter what, do not tell any men we chat up what you do for a living. Not unless we're trying to get away from them."

Cinnia didn't have Vera's interest in meeting men. Her mother's lack of a career to fall back on had been their downfall. All Milly was qualified to do was take in university students as boarders because she had a big house, which was how she paid the bills, much to her everlasting embarrassment. She spun it as a lark when people asked about it. She liked to be surrounded by young people, she said, playing eccentric.

Cinnia was determined never to have her back against the wall like that. She was already self-supporting and, even though she knew running her own agency came with risk, she had hit the ceiling where she was. The next step was to become her own boss.

Thus, she was thinking about how to build her client list as she stood with Vera, chatting to an unassuming musician and a nerdy social-media magnate. The men were ridiculously wealthy and equally shy, which was why bubbly women like Vera had been called in, Cinnia supposed, letting her gaze stray to take in an evening beyond any she would experience again in this lifetime.

The nightclub was in a reclaimed industrial building, tricked out with steel and glass and modern art. Top-shelf liquor was served in cut-crystal glasses by uniformed bartenders. The main room was open to the upper floor, making the place feel airy despite the crush of people in the low-slung chairs and standing in groups around the full dance floor.

Tonight, the tables had been covered with velvet table-cloths and the place was littered with feather boas and faux furs. The typical nightclub black light had been replaced with a sultry red. It threw sexy shadows into every corner and gave faces a warm glow. The DJ was mashing old jazz and modern hits with delightful results while a bouncer guarded stairs that rose to a walk-around gallery on the upper level. When they'd arrived, they'd been given a peek into the ultraposh, private entertainment rooms reserved for the most exclusive guests.

Judging by the movie stars and the other celebrities *not* gaining access, those rooms would be used by a very rich and exalted personality indeed.

Cinnia wasn't impressed with money and fame, but she would love to take on any of these pocketbooks as clients. Sadly, people with this much money to throw around were not interested in a boutique agency still smelling of builder's dust. She had known from the outset that nothing would come of this evening beyond a few lost hours and a cute entry in the logbook of appearances made by her great-granny's tiara. *C'est la vie.*

Then she saw *him.*

Them, really. The Sauveterre twins. The male pair. The same gorgeous man in duplicate arrived at the top of the short flight of entrance stairs, where they overlooked the sunken area of the main lounge.

Her pulse stumbled.

She was startled to see them in person. And curious, of course. She'd been eleven when their sister had been kidnapped, old enough to follow the story as intently as the rest of the world. It had had a profound impact on her. To this day it made her heart feel stretched and tense just thinking about it.

The family name had turned up in a million news stories and gossip magazines and online hits since then. That's how she knew, despite the distance across the dimly lit room, that they were as handsome as they seemed from afar.

They had identical dark hair cut close under matching black fedoras tilted slyly to the left. While every other man had turned up in a baggy, striped suit with a red tie and carried a violin case, these two wore crisp black shirts with the cuffs rolled back, high-waisted, tailored black pants held up with white suspenders and smart white ties.

The sharp look accentuated their muscled shoulders and neat hips, while the narrow cut of the pants drew her eye to their matching black-and-white wing tips. They *looked* like gangsters of old, but the really dangerous ones. The ones so powerful and commanding, they didn't have to swagger. They killed with a blink.

They wore exactly the same expression of bored tolerance as they pushed their hands in their pockets and scanned the room.

It was funny to see them move in unison, which held her attention until one stopped. He turned his head from the direction of the stairs, barely moving, but it was as if he sensed her attention and met her gaze all the way from across the club.

Cinnia's heart took a funny bounce. She told herself it was the embarrassment of being caught gawking coupled with the shock of recognizing a celebrity. Catching a glimpse of the Sauveterre twins, even in a place filled with faux royals and rock stars, was a big deal. She knew they were regular people underneath the reputation, not something to get fluttery over, but she was rather giddy holding this man's gaze.

There's my rich husband, Mum. The thought made her smile at herself.

His head tilted just a little and he gave a slight nod. It was a very understated acknowledgement. *Hello*.

"Who do you see?" Vera asked, and followed Cinnia's gaze, whispering under her breath, "Oh, my *gawd*."

The men moved down the stairs onto the dance floor, leaving Cinnia swallowing and trying to recover from something that had been nothing. Why did her blood feel as though it was stinging her veins?

"We have to meet them," Vera insisted.

"Shh." Cinnia protested, forcing her gaze back to the crooner. She and Vera were supposed to be circulating and making small talk. "Who needs another Gin Rickey?" she asked the men.

She absolutely refused to look around and see if *he* looked at her again. Why would he? Still, she remained attuned to him, feeling prickly and hypersensitive, like she was in grade school and her first crush had entered the room. She knew exactly where he was as they both moved around the room for the next half hour.

Vera leaned into her. "They're by the bar. Let's get into their line of sight."

"Vera."

"We'll just see if we can say hi. Besides, there will be a stampede for drinks when it's time to toast. We should freshen ours now, so we can take them outside for the fireworks."

She and Vera quickly realized they'd be swimming upstream trying to get nearer the twins *or* the bar. They moved to safer ground near the bottom of the stairs and stood with attentive expressions as the club owner quieted the room and thanked everyone for coming.

Or rather, Cinnia gave their host her polite attention while Vera visually cruised for fresh prospects.

Vera would flirt with anyone. She was fun loving, pretty

and had a knockout figure that reeled men in from across a pub or wherever she dragged Cinnia for a night out. They'd met at university and Vera was not only loyal, funny and caring, but also the absolute best at keeping Cinnia from becoming the stick-in-the-mud that Vera always called her.

Cinnia wasn't as curvy as Vera, but she drew her share of male attention. She might not try to get by on her looks the way her mother thought she could, but she knew her wavy blond hair and patrician features gave her certain advantages. They were also a perfect foil for Vera's darker looks, which *Vera* used to her advantage.

Cinnia didn't date so much as play Vera's wingwoman. She had come out tonight knowing they would very likely wind up departing the club with whomever Vera had set her sights on. But, while Vera often went home with men she barely knew, Cinnia fully expected to find her way back to their flat alone.

As the speeches finished up and the fireworks were promised to start soon, there was a minor lull in noise.

"It'd be nice if we could find some men to buy us a drink."

It was classic Vera, spoken mostly in jest because she knew it got under Cinnia's skin. She knew Cinnia believed women should be self-reliant and not look to men for anything.

Cinnia bit back her knee-jerk lecture on feminism, refusing to let her friend get a rise out of her.

Behind them, a male voice said, "Ladies? Are you going up?"

Henri recognized the blonde as they made their way toward the stairs. She had a serene profile and a graceful figure draped in a vintage-style dress that he imagined his sisters would coo over. They were the fashion aficionados, but he knew quality when he saw it.

Everything about this woman was understated elegance. In a sea of heavy makeup and over-the-top flapper gear, she wore a short black number that shimmered with fringe. Her hair was pressed into the pinched waves of old and a simple line of diamonds banded it. One side of her delicate tiara was bedecked with a leafy filigree and a single feather.

She looked smart and feminine without even trying.

She had smiled at him earlier, which was nothing new. People stared and acted like they knew him all the time. Heads in the crowd were turning to do it now. He usually ignored it, but he had looked back at her for a full thirty seconds because, why not? She was beautiful. It hadn't been a chore.

Neither was this side of her. The dress didn't need to hug her figure to show off her pert ass and slender thighs. It was rather erotic in the way it only suggested at the curves it disguised.

"Company?" he suggested.

Possessing exactly as healthy a libido as Henri, Ramon followed his gaze, saw the stacked brunette beside her and commented, "Good eye."

They easily operated as one unit without preplanning. Henri paused beside the women in time to hear them wish for a man to buy them drinks.

Ramon stepped past them to open the chain on the bottom of the stairs himself, not bothering to identify himself to the bouncer. Everyone knew them on sight.

"Ladies? Are you going up?" Ramon's gaze flicked back to Henri. He'd heard their lament and Henri very subtly signaled he didn't care.

They were targets of gold diggers all the time. They had

both learned to take care of themselves. It didn't mean a good time couldn't be had by all.

The brunette blushed and smiled, standing taller, shoulders going back. She was dazzled and very receptive. "Yes. We are." She nodded confidently despite the fact they all knew who moved freely up these upstairs and who did not. She nudged the blonde.

The blonde pursed her mouth with dismay. Embarrassed at being overheard as a mercenary? No need. Henri found that to be the easiest and most convenient of traits to manage in a woman.

The music started up again, increasing his desire to leave the noise and crowd behind.

The blonde looked warily between him and his brother, giving Henri the sense she was trying to work out which one of them had met her gaze earlier.

He and Ramon didn't fight over women. There was no point since neither of them wanted long-term relationships. Women seemed to view them as interchangeable anyway. But Henri found himself annoyed by the idea she might decide to go with Ramon.

What had been a generic restlessness responding to the gaze of a beautiful female ticked up into a desire to have this one in particular.

"Watch the fireworks from our suite," Ramon said with easy command, waving an invitation. "Save me from staring at my own face."

"Why would you stare at your brother when you'll be watching the fireworks?" the brunette asked with a cheeky bat of her lashes. "Maybe if you didn't dress alike you wouldn't feel like you were talking into a mirror?"

"We don't do it intentionally." Ramon offered his arm to escort her up the stairs. "It happens even when we're half the world away from each other. We've stopped fighting it."

"Really!"

The pair was quickly lost in the shadows of the gallery.

The blonde gazed after her friend, biting her lip, then relaxed her mouth and licked her lips as she glanced at Henri. It almost seemed a nervous response, but the action flooded color into a mouth that now looked dewy and soft as rose petals, shiny and kissable. A very enticing move.

His gaze lingered on the sight, as his mind slid naturally into the pleasant fantasy of crushing her mouth with his.

"Shall we?"

She fell into step beside him.

This was not his first time picking up women with his brother. He and Ramon had long ago concluded that if they were saddled with being *the Sauveterre twins* they were damned well going to take advantage of the one outstanding benefit. Startlingly good looks, times two, along with buckets of money and celebrity status meant that the sweetest companions were in endless supply.

"Was that true?" the blonde asked, leaning in to be heard. "That you dress alike at other times, not just tonight?"

"Yes." Henri hated talking about himself and loathed even more talking about his family, but this was one of those innocuous tidbits that strangers loved to hear. The mystery of being a twin was infinitely fascinating to those who weren't. He accepted it and had stopped fighting it, as well.

At least tonight it gave him an excuse to hold her arm as he leaned down to speak in her ear, liking the silken brush of her hair against his nose as he inhaled a scent that was cool English roses and warm woman.

"In fact, when one of us changes out of what the other is wearing, we inevitably spill something and have to go back to the first outfit."

"You're joking."

He shrugged off her skepticism. His sisters were connected on an emotional level. He and his brother were more outwardly aligned. They had very different personalities, were competitive as hell with each other, but often spoke in unison or followed a similar thought process, inevitably arriving at the same end result. As Henri had been calling his brother to suggest they host this year's planning sessions in London instead of their usual Paris or Madrid, Ramon had been accepting the invite to this club opening.

"I'm, um, Cinnia. Whitley." She offered her hand as they arrived on the upper floor.

"Henri." Her skin felt as soft as it looked and was warmer than the pale tone suggested. She had a firm grip for a woman. He didn't want to let her go, but she pulled her hand free to glance behind him at Guy, who had followed them, then frowned at Oscar ahead of them, already stepping through the door to the suite where Ramon waited with her friend.

"Do you have bodyguards?"

"It's just a precaution." They followed into them the suite.

While Oscar inspected the room, Guy brought out his phone and sent a brief text—a request for a background check on both women no doubt. Helping Guy along, Henri introduced himself to the brunette, learning her name was Vera Phipps.

Aside from relying on men's wallets rather than their own, Henri judged both women to be harmless. Vera sent a "jackpot" look to Cinnia when a butler arrived to take their order, then she followed Oscar's path through the room, trailing fingers on the low-slung sofa and chairs as she circled, glancing to the flat screen hung on the wall, and stepped onto the balcony for a quick sniff of the air off the Thames.

She came back just as quickly to fetch one of the swag bags from the coffee table. "Oh! A gold one! Everyone below got silver. And yours is bigger."

"I hear that a lot," Ramon said with a smirk, making Vera laugh throatily.

"I bet you do. May I look?" She batted her lashes suggestively.

Cinnia did not flirt so blatantly. She offered a demure thank-you as the butler poured their champagne and moved outside to glance at the colored lights swirling on the water. In the middle of the river, the technicians on the float set off a test flare.

It was a warm evening without a breeze. Her gaze lifted to the sparkle of lights across the water and up to the stars.

"I'm surprised you stayed below as long as you did when you had this to retreat to," she said as Henri padded out to join her. He was compelled. Drawn. It was strange and not something he would typically indulge. The strength of his attraction made him a little uncomfortable.

Below them, people began filing out to the outdoor lounge while the music followed them.

Ramon was the one who liked crowds. Henri preferred a quieter atmosphere, but he said smoothly, "Good thing we did or I wouldn't have met you."

Her snort was delicate, if disparaging. Most blondes with blue eyes played up the suggestion of vulnerable innocence in their coloring. Not Cinnia. Her vintage hairstyle framed her face in a waifish way, but her brows had a sharp, intelligent angle. Her lashes stayed low and her gaze watchful, not cynical, but not goggling or overly impressed by any of this.

He liked that sign of inner confidence and strength. It

was compelling, sparking his curiosity. "You feel differently?"

"I feel this is a well-oiled machine you two are operating." She flicked her glance to the plate of canapés that appeared like magic on the glass table next to them.

"I would call that distrustful," he said, waiting until the server had gone to swing his gaze back to hers. "If I didn't think you two were running a similar routine. I'll call it hypocritical instead."

Her blue gaze flashed to his, but inside the suite, Vera was laughing at something Ramon had said. The two were meshing like cogs rolling against one another to turn out a foregone conclusion. Cinnia's mouth tightened.

"Unable to deny it?" he taunted gently.

"You approached us," she reminded with enough pique to amuse him.

"I was invited."

"I didn't mean to stare." Her gaze returned to the view, chin coming up.

It had been more than a stare. She had smiled at him.

He watched with fascination as the fringe across her breasts quivered under an indignant breath. He would bet her cheeks were pink if the light was high enough to tell.

"I doubt I'm the first to be curious about the pair of you. You make a fetching couple." Her smile was pure aspartame.

Her eyes, however, were a spun sugar blue. That was unmistakable as a huge white light swirled down from a helicopter, rousing the crowd below into cheering.

Her beauty gave him a sudden kick in the chest. It wasn't a trick of makeup because she wore very little. The requisite eyeliner made her eyes stand out, but she'd only darkened her lashes a little. They weren't lengthened with false ones like so many women wore these days. A shimmery blue streaked across her lids, but otherwise her features were clean and her skin fine and creamy.

"Did you really know it was me who looked back at you, or is that an assumption? Because it usually takes people months, even years to tell us apart." It was easy once a person realized Henri was left-handed and Ramon right, or that Henri tended to speak French as his default while Ramon preferred Spanish, but few noticed those details.

"You are remarkably alike, but..." She glanced into the suite, to where Ramon was holding open the designer bag, listening politely to Vera wax in delight over the contents. They usually let their mother pick over the contents of those bags, then handed the rest to their PAs, but Henri was just as happy to let these women take them home.

He took advantage of Cinnia's distraction to glance at his phone. The bullet points backed up what he'd already assumed. Her mother was wellborn, but the family was broke. Cinnia worked for a wealth management firm and was listed on their website as an intern. Filing and fetching coffee, he assumed. The only risk Cinnia Whitley posed was financial and he was quite sure he could afford her.

He tucked his phone away, irritated to note she was still eyeing his brother, brows pulled together in consternation.

"But?" he prompted, having to stand close to be heard over the music below.

"I don't know. I don't read auras or anything like that, but... Never mind." She flashed him another look, this one self-conscious.

Sexually aware?

"That's interesting." His annoyance evaporated, replaced by intensified attraction. He leaned his elbow on the rail so he was even closer to her, edging into her space, liking the way she tried to quell a little shiver. She smelled like roses and tropics and something earthy that further turned him on.

"Wh-what is?" She was trying to look blasé, but he knew the signs of physical magnetism. There was a pulse beating fast in her throat, but it wasn't fear. She wasn't moving away. She was skimming her gaze across his shoulders and down his chest.

Chemistry was such a wonderful thing. He didn't move, allowing the primal signals to bounce between them, stimulating him and heightening his senses. Sex was the cheapest and best high in the world as far as he was concerned.

"You react to me, but not to him."

"I didn't say that!"

"Didn't you? My mistake."

"You *are* mistaken," she assured him hotly. "Whatever you're thinking about me—*us*—and why we came up here, forget it."

She wasn't used to being so attracted to the men she exploited, he surmised. Poor thing. This must be very disconcerting for her. With that reserved personality, he bet she usually did quite well at stringing a man along. Was she afraid she wouldn't be able to hold out with him until she had squeezed all she could from him?

"I'm thinking you're here to watch the fireworks. What did you think I was thinking?"

She spun back to the view, setting her chin.

He smiled. "Listen." He very lightly stroked the back of his bent finger down her bare arm, entranced when goose pimples chased the same path.

She shot him a look that was startled and uncertain, quickly rubbing the bumps away.

"I don't have to work this hard to get a woman to sleep with me. This is how I live." He waved his champagne glass at the opulence around them. "Enjoy it without feeling obligated."

"You won't expect anything after?" she scoffed.

"By *anything*, do you mean that?" He thumbed to where Vera was on tiptoe inside the suite, painting herself against Ramon, lips firmly locked over his.

Cinnia made a pained noise and looked out across the river again. As strategies went, her friend was overplaying her hand.

"I shall remain hopeful," Henri drawled.

"Yes, you will remain that way," Cinnia assured him.

He hid a silent laugh behind the glass he lifted to his lips, deciding he wanted her quite badly and was willing to pay whatever it cost. He respected people who knew what they were worth.

But he only said, "Don't make promises unless you can keep them, *chérie*."

CHAPTER TWO

VERA, THE *TRAITOR*, left with Ramon before the fireworks started.

"That's what you two were talking about in Spanish?" Cinnia hissed as she had three seconds alone on the balcony to react.

"I told you a language degree opened doors," Vera joked, then rolled her eyes at the face Cinnia was making. "Come *on*. Look at them! Surely you're tempted? It's long past time you worked Avery out of your system, you know."

She knew. And, of course, she was tempted. She wasn't in Vera's league when it came to sexual gymnastics, but she'd had a couple of long-term relationships that had been nice until they'd gone bad. The first had been an immature thing that should have ended before they went off to separate universities, but she'd clung to what they'd had and he'd wound up cheating. Her heart had been battered at the time, but looking back she knew they'd been far too young for the level of commitment she had expected.

Avery, however, had broken her heart in two, professing love for her while they'd both been struggling through a heavy course load and then trying to make ends meet when they moved to London together. Then he had come into some money and cut her off cold, stating bluntly that her family was too much of a handful and he didn't need the dead weight. Thankfully Vera had been there for her when he'd kicked her out.

Since then, Cinnia had stayed out of the relationship arena, thinking it wiser to concentrate on getting her career off the ground.

Not that Henri would offer a relationship. She knew *that* without asking. But she couldn't deny she was intrigued by him. Every time he glanced at her with male appreciation oozing out of his pores, her hormones swayed in an erotic dance of come-hither. Like the extravagance of the night itself, she kept trying to rationalize indulging in whatever he was offering.

She didn't do one-time hookups, though. And even if she did sleep with him purely for the fun of it, he would *believe* she'd done it in exchange for being wined and dined here in this heavenly suite. She hated the idea of him thinking she could be bought. It went right to the core of the insecurities Avery had instilled in her.

"It's quite a signature for the autograph book," Vera murmured with a self-satisfied grin. "You know your mother would approve. There's a first-class trip to Australia in that bag, you know. And a smartwatch and a year's lease on a sports car. Get what you can out of it!"

Henri came back from taking a call, probably overhearing Vera's vulgar suggestion—like he needed any more ammunition to believe they were a pair of opportunists.

Seconds later, Ramon came out and said, "The car is waiting. Lovely to meet you, Cinnia."

He and Vera disappeared like a snuffed flame leaving a wisp of burned friendship hanging in the air.

Henri sat down across from Cinnia at the high-top table, mouth relaxed, but she had the sense he was laughing at her ill-disguised panic. He signaled to the butler to freshen their drinks.

"Where do you think he's taking her?" she asked as the butler left.

"The nearest hotel with a vacant room, I imagine."

She shouldn't have asked.

"Why does it bother you?"

"It doesn't."

"You're judging," he accused. "Why?"

She wanted to deny it. She considered herself open-minded and forward thinking. She didn't slut-shame. Women had needs and Vera was no one's victim.

"Vera can do whatever she wants. I don't like the idea that you're judging me by her choices, though." She hated it. Avery's awful accusations came back to her and she felt raw all over again. Worse even, as she thought of this man who *lived like this* thinking she wanted a shortcut to the same lifestyle. "I don't sleep with men for a swag bag. I have a job. I buy what I need and if I can't afford something, I live without it."

"What do you do?" He looked like he was asking out of politeness, not like he really believed her speech on self-sufficiency.

She almost blurted "funeral arrangements" just to put him off.

"I have a business degree and I'm a qualified financial advisor, but my focus is estate planning and trust management."

His stall of surprise was painful in how loudly it spoke of his having underestimated her.

"I'm a very boring person," she said, wishing she could be more smug at defying his assumptions about her, but she only felt the difference in their stations more keenly. He had obviously written her off as trifling. And yes, she was trying to climb higher than where she'd wound up, but through honest hard work. Still, she would never reach his level and that put *him* well beyond her reach.

Not that she wanted him.

Did she?

With an uncomfortable sting in her blood, she picked up her champagne then remembered she had decided to stop drinking now that Vera was gone. She took a sip of water instead.

"I wasn't expecting that," he admitted.

"You thought I was a secretary? Airline hostess? Model? Even if I was, those are all honest careers in their own right."

"They are. And you could model. You're very beautiful."

"So could you. You have a face so nice, God made it twice."

He snorted. "Point to you," he conceded with a grimace. "I absolutely hate to be reduced to 'one of the Sauveterre twins.' We are all more than we appear on the surface, aren't we?"

Oh, the bastard, now she couldn't hate him unequivocally.

"Is it bad?" she asked, feeling compelled to do so. "I mean, I see things online all the time that I know have to be pure rubbish. The same nonsense that shows up about all celebrities, saying you're having an alien's baby or whatever. Does it bother you, though? Do you resent being famous because of an accident of birth?"

He took a moment to answer.

"I don't resent being who I am. I don't talk about my family—" his gaze shot to hers in warning to stay well back "—but I wouldn't trade them for anything. The attention is a pain in the ass and not something we invite. It annoys me, but I've learned to pick my battles." He said it flatly, but the nail beds of his fingers were white where he gripped his glass.

"Well, I—" She stopped herself, holding out a hand. "Message received about your family," she assured him. "You've earned the right to privacy. But I hope she's well. Your sister, I mean."

She was tempted to say more, weirdly yearning to explain that his family's pain had rippled out to her in the strangest way. She'd been as taken as anyone with the Sauveterre twins. The girls were a little younger than her, but they had seemed like an ideal worth emulating, living much larger than Cinnia even though her family had been doing quite well in those days.

Then Trella had been kidnapped and she'd been terrified for the girl. Of course, she had been compelled to follow the rest of the family's exploits forevermore. She was as curious as anyone about why his youngest sister had dropped out of the public eye in her teens. Had she gone into rehab? A madhouse? A nunnery? Theories abounded, but Cinnia kept her lips sealed against asking for the truth.

Against asking him if he was still dealing with the fallout.

The butler brought another plate of hors d'oeuvres, this one with tiny deviled quail eggs, caviar and stuffed olives and a whipped salmon mousse with narrow fingers of toasted bread. It was exquisite and she kept her gaze on it to hide how thinking of his past had altered her perception of him. She wanted to dismiss him as a womanizer who should be avoided, but he was human. He'd been hurt. Scarred.

"Why estate planning?"

She dragged her gaze off the plate, heart taking a skip as she met his gaze.

"Many reasons. I started looking into it after my father died. There was a lot to untangle and as I learned what he could have done, I kept wondering why he hadn't set it up this way or that. My mother would have had it easier if he'd shown some foresight. Looking at it as a career, I saw it was flexible, something you could do without a lot of overhead. You can even work from home if you have to. Everyone needs a will, whether they know it or not. And it's one of those things that if you're good and fast, you can make a decent living. I didn't see a downside beyond its lack of sex appeal."

"Which you more than make up for in being yourself."

He said it with gentle mockery. She knew he meant it as over-the-top flattery, but her cheeks still warmed. She tried to hide how affected she was with a dry "I try."

The fireworks started and they turned to watch.

She was more aware of him than the performance. He was very charismatic with his air of aloof charm and hint of a French accent. He was also subtly demonstrative, lightly caressing her wrist as he drew her attention to the flotilla of boats coming in to watch.

Everything he did made her very aware of herself. Her breaths felt deliberate, her skin sensitized, her movements a dance of grace. She was being seduced and he wasn't even making an effort to do it. Her mind drifted to thoughts of kissing him. Feeling his weight against her.

Her skin warmed, her nipples tingled and she pressed her knees together to ease the ache in the fork of her thighs.

She was sorry when the fireworks ended and her excuse for being here was over.

"Oh, no," she said quickly, declining the butler's offer to bring strawberries and cream with a fresh bottle of champagne as he removed their plate of finger foods.

"Do *not* worry about your figure," Henri said, nodding to the butler.

"I'm worried about my *survival*. I'm allergic. I have a pen for emergencies and everything." She nodded at her clutch.

"It's that bad?" He held up a hand to halt the butler.

"I nearly died at a sleepover once, because my friend didn't want to fess up that she'd stolen a bottle of her dad's best wine for homemade sangria." She rolled her eyes, making light of what a frightening near miss she'd had.

He refused the strawberries and told the butler he would press the call button when they were ready for more champagne.

"Have them if you want them," Cinnia protested. "It's not so bad I can't watch someone else eat them."

He tucked his chin, leaning forward as the butler closed the door behind himself. "But I can't kiss you if I've eaten them. Can I?"

His words made her ears ring. She stole a long, subtle inhale, holding his gaze while she tried not to let him see how easily he sent her blood pressure into the stratosphere.

"Remaining hopeful?" Her gaze dropped to his mouth.

"Very much so."

She forced herself to slide off her tall chair, excusing herself to the attached powder room. *Time to go*, she told her reflection. The woman in the mirror was entirely too heavy lidded, her defenses against Henri thinning by the second.

When she returned, Henri was inside the suite. The lighting fell in subdued angles off the wall sconces and from the patio lanterns below the balcony, setting an intimate tone while the music inside the club pulsed in muted rhythm through the walls.

Henri had raided his swag bag for a box of chocolate

truffles with a Belgian label and was opening one wrapped in gold foil. A ball of discarded foil was already on the table next to the box.

"I have a sweet tooth," he admitted ruefully, offering the truffle.

"No, thanks. I'll, um, go. This was nice. Thank you." She stuck out her hand, feeling like an idiot the moment she did it.

He set aside the chocolate and brought out his phone. "I'll order the car and take you."

"I can manage."

He gave her a pithy look. "I meant it about not feeling obligated. I can drive you home without attacking you. I've made my appearance here. I don't plan to stay."

It wasn't him she was worried about. She was half-tempted to ask him to find the nearest vacant hotel room. Vera's voice was playing in her head, extolling the virtues of being a modern woman who owned her sexuality. *You eat if you're hungry, don't you?*

Cinnia was sexually hungry. She put it down to the excitement of dressing up for an extravagant evening, the soft breeze caressing her skin and champagne relaxing her. Henri was very attractive and she would bet any money he easily satisfied the most exotic of appetites.

"I think it's best if we end it here." She felt like a coward and couldn't help looking at his mouth again. She wanted him to kiss her. She really did. Her blood thickened in her arteries, throbbing with anticipation.

He quirked his lips. "If you tell me you have an allergy to chocolate, I'm going to be disappointed."

"I'll survive," she murmured, recognizing that she was consenting to a kiss. "My affairs are in order if I don't. And what a story to tell my grandchildren if I do." She said it to be cheeky, to keep this light and disguise that she was intrigued by him.

His breath rushed out in an incredulous *ha*, but he wasn't deterred. He crowded close, hands opening on her waist and drawing her forward into him.

"I'd best make it memorable then."

She wore low kitten heels and he was very tall, well over six feet and overwhelming as he bent his head to brush his mouth against hers.

She clutched his shoulders for balance, shivering lightly, head instantly swimming. Was that it? She swallowed and wet her lips then parted them, inviting a more thorough goodbye than that.

He started to smile and she knew his move had been a deliberate tease to make her want more. He moved in like a damned marauder then covered her mouth fully, angling to plunder. *Claiming*.

She curled her fingers against his shoulders, feeling them tense as he drew her closer. She moaned as she kissed him back, quickly over her head and suddenly drowning. He buffeted her senses, filling her brain with the faint scent of aftershave and masculinity, enfolding her as she melted under a flood of arousal. His tongue came into her mouth and she tasted dark chocolate and darker intention.

He wanted her. She could feel how hard he was against her stomach. Her own body grew hot and achy in seconds. Longing struck her loins and she looped her arms fully around his neck to mash her breasts against his chest.

Too much, she thought as she did it, knowing it was a signal of receptiveness, but it was pure instinct. Wanton need.

She drew back, gasped once for air, then found herself kissing him again. Just once more. Okay twice. The third time she might have found her willpower, but the solidness of a wall arrived at her back. He ran his lips down her throat and slid his hand to cradle her breast.

"Oh," she breathed, loving the gentle way he massaged, then found her nipple through the fringe, circling and teasing. Her knee came up to his thigh of its own accord, making space for him to settle against her aching mons.

He growled his approval and ran his hand up her thigh, taking the hem of her dress up to her waist, hooking his forearm behind her knee and caressing her bottom as she picked her hips up off the wall and met his suggestive thrust.

He kissed her deeply, tongue delving into her mouth as he fondled her breast and the skin of her bottom exposed by her thong. They rocked in mock lovemaking, their sighs too low to be heard over the noise of the crowd and music drifting in from the open doors of the balcony.

This was so not her. She liked sex, but she had never behaved like this. It had never *felt* like this. She might actually climax fooling around fully clothed, grinding herself against him if he kept up that perfectly delicious rhythm. The hard length of him was right where it needed to be, rubbing against her most sensitized flesh. She was *so* turned on and really tempted to let it happen. It was like they were dancing. The song's beat was picking up, growing more intense. Tension was gathering in her abdomen and lower, in the flesh he was stimulating so erotically.

Dropping her head back against the wall, she bit her bottom lip, one hand bracing on his shoulder. They had to stop. They were practically in public and she was *so* close!

He whispered something in French that sounded like encouragement and reached one hand to lock the door. "It's okay. Come."

"I'm not—"

"*Oui, chérie*, you are. Very close. I can feel you trembling. It's exciting. Come."

She wanted to tell him he didn't know how she felt, but he kissed her like he had the first time, barely grazing her mouth so she turned her head, seeking further contact and clinging to his lips with her own.

"Let me give you this," he whispered as he broke away and shifted to bring his hand between them, gently tracing her tender flesh through the damp layer of black silk.

She stopped breathing. Anticipation held her very still as he drew light patterns over the silk of her thong. Her entire being narrowed to the touch of his fingertip, which was so light, yet made her throb with need. She waited in agony for his caress to steal beneath the elastic and…

"Mmm," she moaned when he finally did it.

"You like?" He stroked her *exactly* the way she needed, unhurried, kissing and drawing away, stoking her arousal, kissing her more deeply, gently penetrating, then whispering praise, promising to make it so good for her. "Come. I want you to."

She was going out of her mind, but his control was equally crazy making. She wanted to let go but she couldn't stand that he was doing this *to* her.

"Do you have a condom?" she gasped when he let her breathe again.

He stilled, eyes a silvery glimmer in the low light, gaze burning into hers.

"You want to make love?" he asked on a rasp.

Oh, please. His hand was in her knickers. He knew what she *wanted*. She was dying. But she wanted climaxing to be something they did together.

She slid her hands down to his fly, hands shaking so much with anticipation she was clumsy as she tried to open his pants.

He removed his hand and hooked her thong to peel it down, letting her leg drop so the silk slid to her ankles. Then he shrugged out of his suspenders and finished opening his pants, bringing a condom from his pocket before he hitched his pants low on his hips and revealed himself.

It ought to have been the moment she woke up and realized this was way beyond where it was supposed to go. Across the suite, the doors were open to a crowd of famous faces, hidden just below the rail.

Her world became a narrow, shadowed one where her blood was on fire. Every breath she drew was filled with his spicy, masculine scent. She admired the shape of him in the low light as she watched him roll the condom down his length. She was so filled with anticipation her loins clenched in pangs of yearning.

He nudged his feet between hers, stepping the thong off her ankle as he settled against her again, the heat of his body a type of deliverance. She gathered her skirt and lifted her leg, hooking her calf against his buttocks, offering herself. He bent his knees and glided to caress, teasing her a moment, wetting the tip before he nudged for entry. He pressed, finding no resistance, and thrust smoothly into her slick channel, so she dug her nails into the back of his neck and made a keening noise at the intensity of his thickness filling her.

"Hurt?" he grunted with surprise, pulling back a little.

"Oh, no," she breathed. "So good." She tightened her foot into the back of his thigh, urging him deeper.

He growled a noise of agreement and pressed all the way in, giving her a moment to greet his intrusion with little rippling hugs of her inner muscles, joyous at the invasion of that hot, hard length. So rock hard. They kissed like that, joined, barely moving as they stood against the wall, tongues laving against each other, bodies quaking with holding back, hot, so hot.

She had never been so overcome by desire that she stood against a damned wall with a stranger. She had never felt so desperate for *more*. She nudged to signal him that he was making her wait too long. Her arousal was a screaming pitch of need.

He breathed a soft laugh against her mouth and began to move with heavy purpose, not rough, but thorough, drawing out each movement so the pleasure went to its furthest degree each time, dragging tingles to the tips of her extremities. It was so sweet it made her teeth ache. She kept thinking it couldn't possibly get better, then he thrust heavily, landing deep, and it was fantastic.

She ceased thinking about where she was or who he was. Their lovemaking became her entire focus. Nothing mattered except that he was moving within her in that exquisitely perfect way. It was earthy and uncivilized, yet so finely tuned it was art. She wanted him with her in this place where he'd propelled her, where nothing existed except this pleasure.

She ran her tongue up his neck and sucked his earlobe and angled to take him as deeply as she could. She kissed him back with abandon and brought his hand up under her dress to her breast, then slid her own under his shirt to caress his tense stomach. She whispered, "I can't believe we're doing this."

He said something in French, his whole body shaking, as though he was in the same state of straining to hold back because this was too good to release.

"You're killing me, *chérie*. I can't hold on. Are you ready?"

"I don't want it to end," she gasped, turning her open

mouth against his neck and gently biting as the crisis threatened.

"Neither do I, but—ah!"

"Yes. Oh, Henri."

"Oui. Ensemble. Maintenant." He thrust harder. Faster.

Glory rose up in a gathering wave, locking them together in ecstatic culmination.

CHAPTER THREE

IT WAS WEEKS after the nightclub before Henri found himself in London again. He hadn't stopped thinking about Cinnia Whitley and he didn't know why. Their evening together had followed exactly the pattern he'd assumed it would and it wasn't a new one.

Well, he usually closed an encounter with more grace, but she was the one who had disappeared when he'd stepped away to take what he thought might be an emergency call from his sister.

Regardless, it wasn't as if Ramon was giving a second thought to her friend Vera, so he didn't know why he couldn't stop thinking about Cinnia. Maybe it was because she hadn't behaved as predictably as her friend.

Vera had posted the selfie she'd taken with the four of them when they'd first entered the hospitality suite. She was using her rub with a Sauveterre to gain some celebrity status of her own. Absolutely nothing new and he didn't even bother feeling disgusted by it.

Cinnia hadn't shared the selfie to her own account, though. The one online quote he'd found attributed to her about him was "I met him briefly. There's nothing else to say."

Not one to kiss and tell, obviously.

Neither was he, so he appreciated her discretion.

Of course, what could one say about their lovemaking without sounding like a blatant liar or an overly romantic poet? He liked an involved partner and always did what he could to ensure the woman got as much from their lovemaking as he did. But to say he and Cinnia had had sex, or had given each other an orgasm, was to completely understate the act.

He kept rationalizing what had made it seem so powerful. She'd been resisting their attraction in a slow burn that had made her capitulation all the sweeter. The partially public location had held a titillating appeal. Their chemistry was very compatible.

As he'd leaned against the soft cushion of her body, barely able to keep his knees from buckling, he'd been… He wanted to call it empty, but even though he'd felt drained, he'd also felt utterly satisfied.

At peace.

All the responsibilities that weighed on him were still there. He hadn't stopped caring about them, but in that moment of euphoria, he'd accepted it all. If that was what had made him into the man who could be there with that woman, forehead tilted against the wall, cheek pressed to hers, inhaling her scent and twitching with reaction long after the pulses of orgasm had faded, feeling the very light stroke of her fingertips at his spine…

So be it.

Then he had heard Trella's ringtone and his demanding life had rushed back in to consume him. He had stepped away from Cinnia and straightened himself, snatching up the phone and answering it without visuals, stepping outside in case Trella was in crisis and he needed to talk her down.

Looking back, he knew he had reacted almost like a shock victim, rushing to get on with his life after a collision that had nearly taken his life. His head had been spinning, his body firing with adrenaline.

Since then, he had been telling himself he was wrong. Their lovemaking hadn't been anywhere near so profound as he recollected. Even if it had been the best sex of his life with a woman who possessed an ounce of discretion, so what? He wasn't in the market for a relationship and given the life he led, never would be.

At best, he might have stretched their association into the rest of the weekend, if she hadn't disappeared like the fire bell had rung. When he had realized she hadn't just ducked into the ladies' room, he had told himself it was for the best and asked for his order of strawberries.

The berries had been both sweet and tart, imprinting on his memory a little deeper with each bite. He suspected he would think of her every time he glimpsed a strawberry for a very long time and would wonder if she was managing to stay away from them.

Why? Such a ridiculous question to clog up his brain.

And yet, weeks later, as he entered a party he had no desire to attend and spotted her, his first thought was *so far so good*. She was alive and well, not having succumbed to fruit poisoning.

Her blond hair was gathered in a knot and held in place with a couple of sticks, but a few delicate spirals fell around her face. Her shoulders were bared by her white summer dress, her heels an attractive spike that showed off her legs. She wore only a pair of silver hoop earrings for jewelry.

She was as casually beautiful as he remembered, her expression serene as she listened to a man who wasn't her date, but looked like he wanted to be.

As was his habit, Henri had insisted his security be given the finalized guest list before he accepted the invitation. If people wanted him to show up to their affairs, they complied. That's how he had known Cinnia would be here and he'd made himself take a full ten minutes of sober second thought before he'd accepted the invite himself—without a plus one, as she had also done.

His heart started to thud with male need as he looked at her. He knew what lurked beneath that air of containment and he'd be damned if that gangly pontificator would discover it, as well.

Cinnia had convinced herself this engagement party for her friend from uni was yet another good "networking opportunity," even though she knew why she'd been invited. Once Vera's photo of the two of them with the twins had made the rounds, Cinnia had been inundated by old acquaintances eager to reach out. She was part of the "it" crowd now and her mother couldn't be happier.

If only she was in a position to decline, but she was too practical to be proud. Her friend was marrying into a very wealthy family from New York and their circle of friends included the types of fortunes that were just complex enough to need a qualified manager.

Unfortunately, you couldn't reply to casual questions about your career with "I'm drumming up biz for the agency I'm opening." Evenings like this were about making introductions and impressions, keeping the talk light yet memorable, then somehow finding an excuse at a point down the road to contact the same people and ask, "Do you have a plan for your eventual death?"

Since she didn't have a man in her life who was eager to put on a tie and show up to a stranger's engagement party, she had come alone and was now a target for the stags in rut. Gerald, here, was a perfect example, shadowing her through her last two attempts to ditch him. She swore if he asked for her number, she would give him her business card and tell him to call when he was ready to discuss his final wishes.

"Don't look now, but guess who just walked in," the woman across from her said with a sparkle in her eye. "I think you know him, Cinnia."

Of course Cinnia looked.

And promptly felt stretched thin as a strand of glass, so brittle she would break if a wrong word was breathed in her direction. Her throat closed and her chest stung from the inside. It took everything in her to keep a look of nonchalance on her face while her heart bolted for the nearest exit.

He was looking right at her, gorgeous in tailored grey pants and a black shirt *sans* tie, hat or suspenders. His forest green linen jacket should have looked affected, but, of course, it was a simple statement that he was gorgeous *and* stylish in modern garb as well as vintage.

"Not really," she said, turning back to her group, *begging* her cheeks not to go hot with betrayal. "I only met them briefly," she lied. For the millionth time.

It was an open secret that Vera had slept with Ramon. She hadn't just notched her bedpost, but had engraved the words *A Sauveterre Slept Here* on her headboard. *Everyone* assumed Cinnia had put out as well and it had taken her weeks to convince the world at large she hadn't.

Because, when a man could walk into a room and create a stir without doing a damned thing, what red-blooded woman *wouldn't* sleep with him the first chance she got?

Guilty as charged, obviously, but Cinnia was far too mortified to admit it. Why, why, why had he affected her so strongly she'd gone against her basic principles? She could already feel him creating the same wicked stir in her—which was unconscionable now she understood he hadn't just been availing himself but *cheating*.

"Friends with the groom, I guess?" Gerald murmured. "Looks like it. Not your date then, Cinnia?"

"No," she asserted, refusing to look at Henri again. *Refusing.* Burning inside with rejection. "I'm not even sure which one that is," she said, utterly bald-faced.

But she knew that was Henri. It didn't make sense to her that her body recognized him at a basic level while regarding his brother like any other man, but there it was. She was attuned and susceptible to *this* twin.

Please, God, don't let him know how susceptible. Would it be too obvious if she excused herself to the ladies' room and caught a cab away from here?

"What did you get for the happy couple?" she asked, trying to steer the conversation off Henri. "I saw they'd registered for one of those bullets to make smoothies, but someone beat me to it. I got them the yogurt maker instead."

"He's coming," the woman said, barely moving her lips, then pasting on a big smile. "Mr. Sauveterre. It's so nice to meet you."

"Bonjour." He nodded and set his wide hand on Cinnia's lower back as he leaned in to shake the offered hand. She stiffened, burned by the imprint of his touch through the satin of her dress. "Cinnia. Nice to see you again. Will you introduce me to your friends?"

She could hardly breathe with his palm sending waves of sensual excitement through her.

"Of course, um—" she squinted at him, making a show of guessing "—Henri?"

His gaze flashed and his thumb and finger dug into her waist in a suggestion of a pinch, promising retribution. *"Oui."*

He was a master at the small talk game, asking people how they knew the betrothed couple, discovering occupations and commenting on places of travel without offering a single detail about himself.

She stood dumbly paralyzed by his hand resting against her spine, telling herself to walk away, but unable to. Her entire body was reacting with the tingling memory of his muscled body moving against hers. Within her. It was all she could do not to betray that she was growing aroused by standing next to him. If she walked away, she'd only draw attention to how gripped she was by her reaction.

"Oh, Cinnia, there's someone you should meet. Let me introduce you."

Henri smoothly snagged her hand and drew her away while Gerald stammered, "Nice chatting with you, Cinnia…" in their wake.

Enough. She had to get away. She tugged at her hand. "I'm leaving," she told him.

"Excellent. Me, too."

Oh, nice one. She had walked blindly into *that*.

"But I do have to say hello to this couple." Apparently he knew them from New York. He drew her across the room.

She followed to avoid making a scene and they chatted for a few minutes. Cinnia quietly fumed, hating him and herself for still reacting. She was just about to make her escape by excusing herself to the powder room and crawling out a window when Henri tightened his grip on the hand she was subtly working free of his.

"I'm afraid we have to run. We should say good night to our hosts," he added to Cinnia, exactly as if they were a couple who had arrived together.

"They" were not a couple. He had demonstrated that clearly enough at the nightclub. Growing hot with fresh outrage, she waited until they'd left the prospective bride and groom and their roomful of friends with a meaty chunk of gossip to chew over before saying, "Why are you doing this? You're ruining my reputation."

"Untrue. Nothing a Sauveterre touches turns to anything but gold. You can thank me later."

"How?" she demanded with undisguised bitterness.

"Don't be crass." He steadied her with a hand under her elbow as he walked her down the stairs and out through the lobby of the hotel. A car glided to the curb before them. His guard reached around them to open the back door. "Where can I take you?"

"I think you know where I want you to go. I prefer you go alone."

"So hostile. You can't possibly be upset about how we left things since it was your choice to leave. Let's have this conversation away from our audience."

Flashes started going off and she realized paparazzi were swarming like mosquitos scenting fresh blood.

She slid into the car and he followed, reaching forward to close the privacy screen before the door had been slammed behind him.

His guard moved into the passenger seat and the car pulled away.

"I didn't expect such a cold greeting."

She made a choked noise. "I can imagine how you thought I'd greet you, given the way I behaved, but forget it. That was me getting over an old boyfriend. *That's all.*"

That's what she kept telling herself and she believed it about as well as anyone else believed she hadn't slept with Henri Sauveterre.

"Vraiment?" His tone chilled by several thousand degrees.

"Oh, I'm sorry, do you find that insulting?" She flicked her head around to send him a haughty look. "At least he and I were completely over. I didn't take his call while you and I were still—"

She wouldn't say it. It was too humiliating. Her cheeks hurt with a painful blush.

Giving in to the urge to make love with him on such short acquaintance was a tolerable mistake. Yes, she'd been weak enough to succumb to a player's best moves, but from a purely physical standpoint—pun intended—it had been great. She hadn't had any regrets as he'd leaned against her, both of them damp and still breathing hard.

Then the ring of his mobile had galvanized him into withdrawing and straightening himself, as he grabbed the phone and said, "Bella." He had gone outside, seeking privacy.

He might as well have smacked her. *Of course* he had other women in his life. Maybe their lovemaking had been profound and unique for her, but it was routine for him. She was no more than the stick of gum he chewed for fifteen minutes to freshen his breath!

Cinnia had tugged on her knickers and got the hell out of there.

"Are you serious?" he muttered now. "The call was from my sister."

"Not any less offensive," she declared, turning her disconcerted frown to the window, cautioning herself not to believe him. *Fool me twice...*

"*D'accord.* You're right. It was rude," he said begrudgingly. "But there are circumstances. I don't ignore her calls."

"That's nice. Tell your driver I'm on the other side of London. He's going the wrong way."

"Cinnia," Henri growled. "Have some compassion. There are *reasons.*"

The kidnapping? The isolation? She glanced at him,

desperately wanting to throw his words back in his face, but he didn't look manipulative or even like he was trying to cajole. He looked frustrated and, beneath it, troubled.

She recalled him saying he never spoke about his family and sighed. Perhaps she would have to take him at his word, but it was still insulting as hell.

"Fine," she muttered.

"Do you mean that? Or is it a passive-aggressive *fine*?"

"Does it matter? I could ask you to tell me what those circumstances are, but you're not going to, are you?"

"No." His expression darkened.

She shrugged, hiding that his reticence struck her as lack of trust, which hurt far more deeply than it had a right to.

"So what do you care if I'm fine or not? Even if we'd ended things on a warmer note that night, you were never going to call me after. We both know that, so who cares how we end things now?"

"I care, obviously."

"No, you don't!" she cried on a scoffing laugh. "You walked into that party and saw the easiest girl in the room." If she could take back her capitulation... Would she? Oh, it was lowering to admit it, but probably not. Regardless, she'd be a fool to repeat it.

"You're looking for a do-over," she accused. Her voice cracked and she forced out a tight *no, thanks.*

"Au contraire," he said, his voice so sharp and hard it stabbed through the thick plate she was trying to hold over her chest. "At least three women in that room were far easier. Trust me. I've met them in the past. Not slept with them," he quickly clarified. "But I've been invited to on very short acquaintance. I came tonight because you were on the guest list."

Her emotions were taking a bumpy ride despite the

smoothness of the car's suspension. He'd come to see *her*? She didn't want to believe that. It would make her soften toward him and she was already struggling to keep him at arm's length.

"I wish you hadn't. My supervisor already suggested it would be a good career move if I sent you a letter of introduction for the firm." She turned her face to the window again. "Now he'll be even more of a pain about it. *Thanks*."

"You want me to come into his office and let him give me his spiel? Fine."

"No, Henri, I don't!" She swung her head around, barely able to keep a civil tone. "What message does that send? Next he'll *tell* me who to sleep with in order to land a client. Men! Are you really that obtuse? Your notoriety is not 'gold' for me. It's a scarlet letter. Don't do me any favors."

He sat back, a ring of white appearing around his tight mouth.

"I can't help who I am, Cinnia. I can't help that people want to use me, or use anyone who comes close to me to get to me. If I could change it, I would, but I *can't*!" His voice rang through the small space like a thunderclap, rife with incensed frustration.

His outburst was so shocking, she sat in silence a moment, absorbing what he'd revealed—reluctantly, judging by the way he shut down immediately after.

Empathy rolled into the spaces he'd blown open in her. She couldn't help feeling bad for him then, especially as a motor scooter buzzed up alongside the car and the passenger on the back aimed a camera at the darkened window. It flashed, perhaps catching her frown of dismay.

He pinched the bridge of his nose, making a visible effort to maintain his strained control.

"Trella—Trella Bella as we call her, or Bella—has a particular struggle. Partly it's due to the attention we draw.

I make myself available to her when she needs it. We all do. If she had called Ramon, your friend Vera would be the one feeling slighted. Trella's situation is a fact of my life. That's all I'm saying on the topic and you can believe it or not or post it to your damned news feed if that will make you feel better."

"Of course I wouldn't," she said crossly. "Why would I deliberately hurt someone I don't even know?"

Now she would dwell forever on the struggles of that poor girl who had surely been through enough just from being kidnapped. No public statements had ever been made about what had really happened to her during the five days she was missing. Terrible things had been theorized, though. Cinnia dearly hoped none of them were true, but judging by Henri's grim expression, his sister had a lot to deal with.

She had such an urge to reach out to him in that moment, she had to clench her fingers together in her lap.

"Has the attention been bad?" he asked. "Are you being harassed by cameras outside your home? It's so rare I meet anyone who feels like I do, I didn't imagine it would be a burden for you."

She shrugged. "Mostly just friends and family are asking about it. I didn't say much and that's not out of character because I keep a low profile as a rule."

He glanced inquiringly, so she explained further.

"My kind of work is like banking or the law. Clients expect confidentiality and no one wants to give their portfolio to a woman who's posting party photos or running with a sketchy crowd, so I live quietly and don't put much online. But as you say, people put a lot of stock in the Sauveterre name. I realize it's not really a detriment to be associated with it. It would shatter my ego completely, however, to have people say I only succeeded because of who I know. And to have my boss pressure me like that? I was really annoyed."

"Did you report him to your HR?"

"There's no point."

"There is. Speaking as the president of a huge company, I can't fix what I don't know is broken. I need reports of that sort of thing so I can take action or it will keep happening."

She hadn't thought of it that way, only that she was leaving soon. "Fine. I will."

"Good."

Great. Annoying-boss issue resolved. "Can you take me home now, please?"

"I would like to have dinner with you."

"You don't want dinner, Henri." That damned crack was back in her voice, betraying that she was still feeling slighted because even if he hadn't been cheating when he'd made love to her, it had been nothing more than a casual hookup. "You want to go to bed with me."

"I do," he said baldly, face tightening at her tone. "Tell me you're not interested and I'll take you home. *Be honest.*"

She wanted to look away, but his intense gaze held hers, peeling back her layers of defensiveness as the streetlights flashed by. She knew she was flushing with guilty anticipation. She had managed to hate him for weeks because he had taken his girlfriend's call after their lovemaking, but that's not what he'd done. Her best reason for resisting him was nullified.

She jerked her head around, staring blindly at the passage of headlights and darkened shop windows.

"Ça va?"

"You could have called," she muttered. "You're not going to call tomorrow if I sleep with you tonight."

"Since you'll be with me at breakfast, there will be no need."

She snorted at his arrogance.

"You were not planning to sleep with me that night." Something in his quiet tone made her listen. It was as if he was reflecting fondly and it gave her a small shiver of pleasure because she was part of a memory he was recollecting warmly. "At first I thought it was your game to resist, but you really were intending to leave. You didn't. You were carried away by a kiss and didn't even take one of those silly gift bags on your way out. Yes, I took note of that detail," he said as she swung a scowl at him.

As if she would have sex for a BPA-free water bottle and the latest reality star's brand of lip gloss!

"You went away feeling ill used and I regret that," he continued. "But I am used by women *all the time*. Put yourself in my shoes and imagine how singular and exciting it is for me to have met a woman who not only responds so strongly to me she lost her willpower against *herself*, but doesn't want to write a damned online diary about it. Yes, I want to experience that again. You're damned right I do."

"I don't *like* that I was carried away like that. It makes me feel cheap."

"Cheap! *Why?*"

"Because you expected it. You expected me to behave that badly and I did."

"I *wanted* you to make love with me. I didn't *expect* it. And there was nothing bad about it. You have a real hangup about when it's permissible to have sex, don't you?"

"Yes, all right? I do! I've had two lovers and I thought I loved both of them. I don't have sex with random strangers for whom I feel mostly annoyance."

He blinked once, taking a moment to pick apart her

words. She expected him to take issue with her calling him annoying, but he only repeated, "*Thought* you loved."

She looked away, aware of tension in the hands that had become fists on her thighs, and said nothing.

"Tell me about this boyfriend you were exorcising."

"No." She craned her neck to look past him. They were pulling up in front of a posh hotel. "What are we doing here?"

"We have dinner reservations."

She had eaten exactly one stuffed mushroom cap at the engagement party. She was starving. Nevertheless, she glared at him.

To hide the fact she was scared.

And shamefully thrilled they weren't parting ways yet. This man utterly fascinated her and it was so dangerous. Like swimming in petrol under a rainstorm of flaming comets.

"Why?" she asked, stalling.

"It's a *date*, Cinnia. Surely that doesn't go too harshly against your precious rules for how to behave with a man?"

She looked at her nails. "No, but I have one about providing the lion's share of sarcasm in a relationship. I suggest you take it down a notch or things could become quite scathing."

He tsk-tsked and started to open his door. His guard finished the job, but Henri held out his hand himself to help her out.

Then he kept his fingers firmly entwined with hers as he walked her through the glittering gold-and-glass entrance of the hotel, across the marble tiles and around the lobby fountain, up the red-carpeted staircase and into a restaurant where a harpist played. The maître d' exclaimed delight that she could join them when Henri introduced her.

The moment they were alone, she said drily, "And I

won't feel obligated after this to go upstairs to the room you've booked."

"No," he assured her. "You won't feel *obligated*." He gathered her hands across the white tablecloth and gave her a slow and anticipatory smile. "But I hope very much you'll feel inclined."

CHAPTER FOUR

CINNIA WOKE TO a room that was nearly pitch-black, Henri's arm heavy across her waist. They were naked, front to front, legs entwined. She wanted to press her lips into the smoothness of his shoulder and kiss his skin.

What the hell was she *doing*?

Succumbing to hormones. And charm. Henri was very engaging when he wanted to be. He smoothly deflected from anything too personal, but he was keenly intelligent and had exchanged lively opinions with her on everything from world politics to pop music. He had asked her advice about a point of estate law, which she had thought was pure pandering, but she soon realized he was serious and had to tell him he was better off consulting someone who specialized in international trusts.

Then the evening's trio had arrived and he had taken her to the dance floor and *seduced* her, right there in front of the world. Not that he was obvious about it. Henri was far too subtle for that. No, it had been a light brush of his chest against her breasts, a whisper that she smelled delicious, a brief contact with his hips so she knew he was aroused.

"I can't help it, *chérie*. You have that effect on me," he had said without embarrassment.

Dessert had arrived, a caramel flan they'd shared, but

they hadn't even finished when he said, "Will you come upstairs? I'm dying to kiss you."

They both knew how she reacted to his kiss.

They might have made love in the elevator if his guard hadn't been with them, standing discreetly at the front of the car with his back to them so Henri could steal a first kiss, then a second, longer, more passionate one.

Inside the suite, they'd barely made it to the bed.

How had she been so aroused? Until that moment, he'd barely touched her.

But even as she lay here next to him, thinking about the way he'd hurriedly skimmed away her knickers and covered himself with a shaking hand, she was growing wet and achy. She had been pure butter beneath him, locking her legs around his waist and lifting into his heavy thrusts.

She should go home. She didn't want to do the walk of shame in the morning, not when she already knew the paparazzi were on to them.

But she found herself slithering closer, sliding her legs against his and giving in to the temptation to taste his skin. He smelled sharp and masculine against his neck. His stubble abraded her nose and lips, but in a sexy way that turned her on because it accented how different they were. Female and male, meant to come together like pieces of a puzzle.

"Encore?" he murmured, moving against her, hardening at her first touch.

"What's wrong with me?"

"Not a damned thing, *chérie*. Ah, this," he growled with satisfaction as he trailed his hand between her legs and found her juicy and plump. "I'm addicted. I have to taste you again." He slid down, pressing her legs open.

She moaned at the sheer indulgence of being pleasured by him like this. He made her feel like she was giving him something when she allowed this, which maybe she was because he pretty much took ownership of her. This act lowered her defenses completely so she was without inhibition, ready to beg when he drew back before she'd climaxed.

"I need to be inside you, *chérie*. I can't wait." He rolled her over and brought her onto her hands and knees.

He covered her like a male animal dominating his mate, filling her with a possessive thrust, so deliciously hard where she was soft and needy. One wide hand slid over her breasts, teased her nipples, rubbed her stomach, then fondled where they were joined as he moved in lusty thrusts.

She received him with cries of encouragement and abandon, so caught up in the raw excitement of it, she didn't care who might hear or what he thought of her behavior. When she climaxed, the paroxysm locked a scream in her throat while he shuddered over and around her, his noises guttural and final. She was *his*. Neither of them could deny it.

That was in the dark.

When she woke in the light of day, and recalled all they'd done, she wanted to *die*.

Why, oh, *why* couldn't she resist him?

Henri had been tempted to join Cinnia in the shower when he woke and heard her starting the water, but he forced himself to put a small distance between them while he contemplated a decision that had been rooting a little deeper into his mind with each hour of lovemaking that had ticked by.

He had never had a mistress, had never wanted anything long-term at all. Not since…

The wrenching memory struck like a kick in the stomach, ambushing him as that dark day sometimes did.

Do you love me?

She had been a pretty thing with caramel eyes and a mouth he'd been trying to kiss for weeks. They were cornered in a stairwell and he was flushed with more attraction than he'd ever felt. Suddenly there was Trella, telling him it was time to *go*.

Go, then, he told her. *Little sisters are such a pain*, he had told the object of his affection, as Trella ran off to be stolen by Gili's—their affectionate name for Angelique— math tutor. *I do*, he had assured the caramel eyes as they were given privacy again. At least, he supposed it was love. He grew excited seeing this girl in the distance. He wanted to hold her hand, touch her all the time. He could hardly take his eyes off her when she was anywhere near him.

And then their friend Sadiq had shouted his name, telling him, "Trella's been taken."

He had seen that girl again, after Trella was home and he and Ramon returned to school. She'd tried to talk to him, but he'd avoided her.

After that, if girls and women came on to him, if they wanted to give up their bodies for mutual physical pleasure, fine. But he was never going to make the mistake of letting a female mean something to him. It put him off his game, exposed a flank.

It could cost the life of someone near and dear.

Romantic love, he had determined, was a weakness he couldn't afford.

Taking a mistress, however, was a slightly less dangerous risk.

He presumed, wondering if he was rationalizing.

Dressing in his pants and shrugging on his open shirt, he moved into the lounge, where he called in an order for breakfast, put in a request for the boutiques to send a selection for them and picked up the paper left outside his door.

"Bon matin," he said to Pierre, who had relieved Guy overnight. "Anything I should know about?"

"All the coverage seems run-of-the-mill, but fresh posts are still coming out. We're keeping an eye out."

Henri nodded, thoughtful, as he closed the door.

He'd never taken a mistress for the same reason he refused to marry and have children: the threat of kidnapping. Women who were only briefly linked to his name were not likely to be targeted or used against him. Precautions would have to be extended to Cinnia if he went through with this.

He scanned the headlines, then picked up his phone to see a text from Ramon. A question mark. Obviously he'd seen the headlines and wondered why Henri was seeing that woman from the nightclub again.

Henri ignored it and returned a text from Angelique with a video call.

"Problème?" he asked, continuing in French. "That was a cryptic message. Why are you worried about something you said to Trella about Sadiq? Are they having a romance I don't know about?"

"What? No! Of course not. No, I think he's falling for someone back in Zhamair. Do you know if that's true?"

"He didn't say anything when I spoke to him last." Sadiq might be the best friend he and his brother had, but they did not discuss their love lives. They talked about important things like stock prices and politics.

"Why does that affect Trella?" he prompted.

"I don't know." She frowned in her introspective way and he knew to give her a moment to gather her thoughts. Angelique was a quieter personality, more like him, preferring solitude, while Trella and Ramon were the extroverts. Everything Trella did was full bore, including a nervous breakdown. She had been making him mad with worry since her birth, when she had turned blue in his arms the first time he held her.

He often thought that if it *had* been Angelique outside the day of the kidnapping, and her tutor had called her over, planning to stuff her in his van, she would have waited for Ramon and insisted he hold her hand and come with her. Shyness had been a hurdle for her, but it was a type of self-protection that served her well.

Trella had possessed none of that. She had run headlong over to the tutor, eager to be helpful and say she wasn't Angelique.

They had stolen her despite her kicks and screams, because how effective was a nine-year-old girl against two strong men?

The trauma affected his sister to this day, which made him blind with fury if he didn't carefully drip-feed himself those memories. It made him want to hurry Angelique to tell him how she imagined Sadiq, their friend who had actually helped save Trella, could be a threat to their sister now.

"I was just talking to her about him," Angelique continued as though still gathering her thoughts. "And saying it was bound to happen that he would marry someday, even if he's not in love now. She got really quiet. Now I feel..." She shrugged. "You know. Like she's upset."

"Deeply upset?"

"No." She said the word on a rush of relief. "Normal upset. But I think she's worried that if he did get married, she wouldn't be able to go to his wedding."

"We can cross that bridge when we come to it," he said. "But thank you for telling me."

Trella had been stable for half a year. They were all holding their collective breath that this time she was actually conquering her panic attacks.

He heard Cinnia and glanced up to see her with dry, windswept hair, wearing one of the hotel robes. "I, um, just want my phone." She scurried to where he had set her handbag on a table after finding it on the floor, where she'd dropped it last night.

"Who's that?" Angelique asked.

"A friend." A very beautiful goddess who had done wicked, devilish things with him in the night. He had not misremembered the power of their chemistry. He kept reminding himself he wasn't a man to be led by his organ, but as many times as they'd made love last night, it wasn't enough. That's what he kept coming back to. He wasn't prepared to go another few weeks, let alone a lifetime, without making love to her again.

"Don't run away," he ordered Cinnia before she could lock herself in the bedroom. "I'm finishing up here." To his sister, he said, "I'll touch base with her later. Let me know if anything changes."

He ended the call and stood, still conflicted now his sister had reminded him of the threats they faced daily and their far-reaching effects.

At the same time, his hands rolled of their own accord, silently inviting Cinnia to come to him.

She didn't move, only hugged herself and flicked her glance to his phone. "Who was that?"

"Gili. Angelique. My other sister."

"You're very close to your siblings."

"They're the only people I trust completely."

She looked at her bare toes. "I speak French. I wasn't trying to eavesdrop, but I heard a little."

"And?"

"And nothing." She shrugged. "I feel bad for your sister. I don't imagine something like that is anything you get over. I mean, I still cry about losing my dad and it's been over a decade, but it sounds like she's quite haunted and I'm sorry she's still affected." She glanced up, expression so soft with compassion it cracked things inside him. "I know you lost your father, as well. I'm sorry for that, too."

"You're sorry for a lot of things." Deepening their relationship would come with many types of risk, he realized. Long-term relationships demanded more of this sort of thing. He was not eager to open up to her, but he hated the distance she was keeping between them right now. The physical distance, at least.

"Are you sorry about last night?" he asked, trying to understand why she wasn't rushing into his arms.

"A little," she mumbled.

"Why?" he demanded, not pleased to hear it.

She kept her head down, but he could see her growing red. With embarrassment?

He swore and went to her, tugging her close with gentle roughness so they knocked together and she threw back her head to scowl at him.

The vulnerability in her eyes made his heart swerve. He was not the only one disturbed by the level of intimacy between them. He found himself rubbing his thumbs against her upper arms where he gripped her, trying to offer reassurance.

"We gave each other a great deal of pleasure. That's not something to be ashamed of."

She swallowed and hid her thoughts with a lowered gaze. Her mouth pouted, maybe even showed a hint of bruising from their thousand rapacious kisses.

Oddly, that hint of injury was the turning point, allowing him to make his decision. They needed time so they could pace themselves. Otherwise, they were liable to kill each other.

"I *like* that you held nothing back," he told her. "Quit being shy about it or I'll do all those same things to you right here on the floor in the lounge. In *daylight*."

Cinnia was tempted to scoff and say, "You can try," but she had a feeling he *would*.

And she'd let him.

He started to kiss her, but the knock on the door interrupted. "Breakfast," he said with a small grimace, releasing her to let in room service.

She touched fingertips to her tingling lips, scolding herself for being disappointed. She was achy and exhausted, very tender in delicate places, and all she could think about was how much she wanted to feel his touch on all those sensitized places again.

Other staff came in with the wheeled table of covered dishes. A woman brought an assortment of outfits and held up each in turn for approval.

"Not that one. It's hideous," Henri said as the woman showed them a green dress. "Why does it even exist? That one, the blue. To match your eyes," he told Cinnia.

He accepted a striped button shirt and the boutique owner left clean underthings for both of them. Cinnia waited until everyone was gone to check the price tags.

"You're not paying for those," Henri said, barely glancing up from the plates he uncovered.

"Neither are you. I guess I'm going home in last night's dress."

"You're my guest. I will provide everything you need while you're with me."

Something in her midsection did a little curl and twist, anchoring and panging inside her. *Get what you can.*

"Are you going to join me? Surely you're as hungry as I am."

"Are you going to keep teasing me about it?" she demanded.

"Last night? Did that sound like teasing? I mean it as praise and gratitude." He looked at her and his shoulders relaxed as he gave her a perplexed look. "*Vraiment*, why does it bother you that we spent a night making love?"

He had stripped her bare, not just physically, but down to her soul. She was never going to be the same. He would always be the man who had done those things and made her feel that way and he would always *know* it. *She* would always know it and compare future lovers and feel wistful. Cheated, even.

"I told you," she muttered, moving to sit across from him, absolutely starving from her expenditure of calories, but feeling defenseless and needy. Tired, she assured herself. She was just tired. And filled with impossible yearning. "I don't do this."

"If you think last night was common for me, you're overestimating my libido."

"Oh, I have a healthy respect for that animal, believe me." *Coffee*. She poured a cup for each of them with shaking hands and quickly doctored hers, sighing with her first sip even though it burned her tongue.

When she glanced at him, he was watching her with an enigmatic look.

"You're also underestimating your effect on me. We have a unique connection." He seemed to choose his words very carefully. "We could leave things here and go on with our lives. I would probably call you the next time I was in London. I will optimistically believe you would be available and want to see me."

That was what was killing her right now. She had been able to put him mostly out of her mind after the first time because she'd been angry and genuinely hadn't thought she would see him again. For him to show up and pursue her so blatantly, however, set her up for believing he would do it again in the future.

She would counsel any girlfriend or sister to *never* wait on a man or give him so much power over her personal happiness, but here she sat, looking into her coffee because she didn't want Henri to see that he already held her on the end of a leash and all he had to do was tug for her to come to heel.

That's where her shame was coming from. Her eyes stung and she made herself blink to stem the tears of humility at being his sexual pet.

"What do I assume by your lack of response, Cinnia? That you would be agreeable to that arrangement?"

"I'm not going to hold a reservation for you," she lied, setting her cup into its saucer with a hard clink and a little slosh of coffee over the rim.

"Exactly what I thought you'd say." He braced his elbows on the table, hands loosely linked above his plate. "Much of your appeal for me is that you expect so little of me. You're very independent. But I do not care to take my chances with your accessibility. I would like to propose a different arrangement."

When she glanced up, his gaze was waiting to snare hers. The hazel-green tone was very, very green. Avid in a possessive, masculine way. *Mine.*

Her stomach swooped and she scented danger, yet it was the lofty danger of swinging out on a rope over a cliff on a bottomless lake. Life threatening, but exhilarating.

"A retainer?" she mocked.

"Of a sort. I've never had a mistress, but I begin to see the benefits."

She was knocked speechless. For a few painful heartbeats, she could only stare, then pointed out, "So. Not a proposal. A *proposition*."

Her pulse raced in panic and she looked across the room at the pretty clothes he was already trying to purchase for her.

Get what you can.

"I believe there are websites where women advertise for sponsors. Perhaps start *there*," she suggested thinly.

"I don't want *a* mistress. I want *you*. Look." He waved at the plates they hadn't yet touched. "I can eat plain scrambled eggs and there's nothing wrong with that, especially when I'm hungry, but if I have the option to eat one poached to perfection, delicately spiced and accompanied by a tempting banquet of other flavors, one that not only sates the appetite but is a joy with every bite, why the hell wouldn't I want the quality ones?"

"And since you're used to buying the best, I'm sure you think you can afford the eggs you see in front of you today. In this case, you can't."

"I'm very rich."

"I'd rather go hungry than sell myself."

He made a noise that was decidedly French. "Forget the metaphors and eat the damned eggs before they go cold."

After they'd both taken a couple of bites, he said, "I'm never going to marry. Long-term dating, in the traditional sense, is a false promise I won't make. Women come to me, come *on to* me, at a steady enough rate that I've never lacked for company."

"I kind of prefer the not calling over this turn of conversation." She flashed a humorless smile. "Just saying."

"But if I expect a woman to make herself exclusive to me, I ought to provide something in return."

"Your charm isn't enough?" She blinked in fake shock.

"Have you heard of erotic spanking, Cinnia? Some

women find it pleasurable and deliberately test a man's patience with backchat, looking for a hot bottom." He showed his teeth. "Just saying."

Wicked, evil man. For one second, she thought about that. Started to blush, and told herself to smarten up.

"You want it straight, Henri?" she challenged, stomach twisting. "Not shaken nor stirred? Fine."

She seemed to have no pride where he was concerned anyway. She dropped back in her chair and gave him a hate-filled glare for forcing her to bring up the pathetic mistakes of her past.

"I told you my father left his estate in a mess. We were in dire straits, actually. Really dire. Mum and my sisters have a hard time seeing it, especially Mum. She has this throwback notion that if one of us marries well, all our problems will be solved. You asked me last night what happened with my ex-boyfriend. That's what happened."

"He was rich and didn't want to marry you?"

"Exactly. Except that we'd been poor together, struggling through school and scrambling for rent every month for a year when we moved here to the city. I was actually the one making more money for the first while. I thought we were in love and that we would get married. Then his folks sold a piece of property and said they were going to split the money between their children. It was a few hundred thousand each, enough to make a nice down payment on a good home. I honestly thought he was being cagey for the weeks following the sale because he was shopping for an engagement ring and planning how to propose."

"Non?" He was holding on to a very neutral tone, betraying nothing of what he might be thinking.

"Hell, no! He was telling his parents to hold off doling out his portion so I couldn't put a claim on it, then he siphoned off half of what was in our shared accounts and kicked me out of our flat the day we were supposed to renew the lease."

She looked at her eggs and knew Avery had been dry, white toast at best while Henri was a mouthwatering croissant.

"I know my family is a handful. I know Mum came on strong when she learned his news. She was on the phone calling local churches that *day*. She flat out told him he should sink his money into her house and said we should move in with her. I never would have let that happen, though. I'll never live with her again if I can help it. She makes me bananas."

She crossed her legs and adjusted the fall of the robe, noting her hand was trembling. She was trying hard to keep a grip, but she still felt so *stupid*. She had thought Avery loved her and it had shaken her confidence in herself, in her belief that she could judge a character and even in her belief that she was lovable. Her voice quavered with old emotion and she couldn't seem to steady it.

"Even though he had known me all that time, he wrote me off as only wanting his bank balance. He said I had always known his parents were sitting on that potential, that I had known money would come to him, and that everything I had done was a calculated investment in getting a piece of it. I did know about it. I had counseled his parents on whether it was better to sell the land before their death or leave it as part of their estate. *Because he asked me to.* And I didn't charge them, by the way. Friends-and-family discount." She picked up her fork and stabbed her egg and watched the yolk bleed out.

Henri reached for his phone and said very casually, "What is his name?"

"Jerkface McPants on Fire. Don't bother ordering a hit. He's not worth the bullet."

He set down his phone again. "This is why you're so sensitive about letting me buy you a meal or a dress?"

"Or a hotel room or a favor with my boss or a rental agreement as a mistress. I earn my keep, Henri. I refuse—I absolutely refuse—to become a kept woman. I'm aiming to start my own agency. I will not work my butt off to succeed only to have people say it's because I was sleeping with a sexy French tycoon."

"My sisters are constantly accused of succeeding with their design house because Sauveterre International underwrote it. Do you know how they respond to that accusation?"

"How?"

"By ignoring it. You do not owe explanations to anyone. You certainly don't have to justify yourself to McFacey man. Stop worrying about what he thinks of you. As for opening an agency, I encourage you to send us a business plan regardless of the terms you and I negotiate for our personal partnership. Ramon and I are investors. We invested in Maison des Jumeaux because Trella wrote a solid plan that has exceeded all of our expectations. If yours shows promise, we may extend you a start-up loan. It won't be nepotism. We do not offer friends-and-family discounts. When it comes to money, neither of us is influenced by sentiment or sexual infatuation. That's why we're rich."

He was not joking.

She was crushed by his reduction of her to a sexual infatuation, but suffered an immediate urge to knock his socks off with her business acumen, wanting to secure a loan from him simply for the achievement of it.

She murmured, "I'll think about it," and returned to eating.

He made short work of his plate and freshened their coffee.

"I like the idea of you working for yourself," he said.

"Why?"

"Because I have a very busy life. It would be hard to find time to be together if you had a strict workweek."

"I love the way you talk like I'm going to agree to be your—oh!" She leaned forward with mock delight. "Let's use the French term, shall we? *Courtisane*."

He gave her a flat look that grew into a considering one.

"An educated woman who values herself and her time? One who is not ashamed of her sex drive? *Is* that you, Cinnia?"

She sat back. "You're trying to make it sound like that's all it is. It's not."

"No, it's potentially quite complicated. But seeing as you are so smart, walk through this with me. I am based in Paris, but I travel to New York at least once a month. I have an office here in London. I could work some of my time out of it, perhaps one week a month. Ramon and I would like to expand into Asia, but we're already stretched thin. And I occasionally drop everything to fly home to Spain if my sister needs me. Tell me how much time we'll have together unless you come with me for some of that travel."

"Presuming I want to spend time with you," she said tartly.

"Look at me," he commanded in such a stern voice her heart stalled and her gaze flashed up to his. "Were you there last night? The bed is a pile of ashes, we set it so completely on fire. If you don't want to do that again, fine. Get dressed and leave. I'll never bother you again."

His words spiked through her heart and she found herself pushing to her feet in a rush of pique, catching the wild flare of something in his eyes before she turned away and—

She halted, unable to make herself take another step.

Something hooked sharp and fierce behind her breast-bone. Tears slammed into her eyes. She brought her fists up and pushed the heels of her hands into her clenched lids, catching a shattered breath. She couldn't move. Couldn't walk away from him.

"Idiot," he said behind her, chair scraping before he pulled her back against his chest, strong arms encasing her, but in a way that felt secure and reassuring.

"I don't want to feel this way," she said in a whisper, voice breaking. All of her breaking. She was self-reliant. She didn't need anything from a man.

But she needed *him. This* man. Who offered *things,* not his heart.

"How do you feel? Hmm?" One hand stole into the front of her robe and he cupped her bare breast, flicked her nipple.

She made a noise of pleasure-pain, instantly catapulted into memory and desire, but her nipples were so tender she covered his hand and stilled his caress.

"Sore?" he asked against her ear, nibbling in a way that sent shivers down her nape, all the way to the small of her back.

She arched, pushing her bottom into the hardness at his loins.

"You're going to kill me, Henri. I ache all over and I don't care. I want you anyway."

"Ah, chérie. You're hurting like this because you don't want our time to end. I feel the same." His mouth opened on the side of her neck, delicately sucking a mark into her skin. "But I will be very, very careful with you, I promise."

His free hand went in below the belt and found her naked and slippery, already responding to being close to him. "You like that?"

"You know I do," she breathed, tilting her head to the

side so his kisses could reach all down the side of her neck. "But I don't think I can."

"Come here." He backed up, bringing her with him.

She heard him unzip his pants and turned to see him putting on a condom. He sat in the chair and drew her to straddle him.

"Gently," he murmured, taking it slow as he drew her down.

Even though she was tender, she breathed a sigh of relief when she was seated on him, full of his turgid heat and completely possessed by this terribly wicked sorcerer of a man.

He opened her belt and spread the robe, looking down at her breasts. His hands moved on her thighs and buttocks, caressing without urging her to move. Then he kissed her, gently and sweetly. Slowly and languorously.

"See?" he breathed against her lips. "We don't have to be greedy if we know we have time."

She was greedy anyway, running her hands across his chest to spread his shirt, then placing kisses there, pinching his nipples and feeling his response inside her. She smiled with secretive joy.

And she began to move instinctively, riding him in an abbreviated rock. She was so tender and sensitive she was gasping in moments, squeezing him with her powerful orgasm.

"Magnifique." He stroked her hair back from her face, set light kisses on her cheekbone and brow and the tip of her nose. His eyes were bright green with arousal. "Do you want to stop? I don't want to hurt you."

"You didn't finish," she said in an urge for him to do so, nerve endings coming alive under the fresh stimulation. She was nearly in tears because it was such an intense sensation.

"I will later, when you're feeling better." He cupped her face, thumbs coming together in the center of her lips, then parting to rest in the corners.

"You're shameless, aren't you?" she said on a trembling breath, frightened by his assumption she would be there for him later today and every day from now on. Maybe she would. Right in this second, she wanted to be whatever he needed her to be. "Don't manipulate me through my body's response to yours."

"Now you won't even accept an orgasm given freely? You are a difficult woman to please."

She ducked her head out of his hands and tucked her forehead against his throat, nose to his collarbone so his scent filled her head.

"You won't ever marry me." She didn't know if it was a refusal, an accusation, or merely a statement of terms.

He tensed, but said firmly, "*Oui.* I will never marry you."

She waited for some kind of repugnance to arrive and prompt her to reject him. All she could think was that at least she would have this, him, for a little while. She closed her eyes, still swimming in the high of orgasm while tendrils of fresh arousal wound around her. He was offering a sensual, sexual contract of association, that was all, but it would be such a pleasurable one.

"I want to marry and have children. Someday. I'm not going to give you all of my best years and wonder what happened when you throw me over for a younger model."

His fingers were under the fall of her hair, working upward in a comb to the back of her skull.

"I'll let you go when you're ready for that. You're not searching for those things today, are you? Be with me until you are."

A half sob pressed out of her. Was she really going to agree to this?

"If either of us was willing to give this up, *chérie*, you would have left in the middle of the night."

"I know," she said on a sob of surrender. "Please don't be smug."

"It's not comfortable for me to be this taken by you." He massaged her scalp, holding her in compassionate, irrevocable intimacy. "I am yielding, too."

It didn't feel like it. He was still hard inside her. She moved restlessly, drawing back to nip his chin, then looked into his eyes. "I bet I'll get there before you do."

"I bet I'll make sure of it." He threw himself forward, swooping her to the floor beneath him, sending them both soaring with the masterful thrust of his hips.

CHAPTER FIVE

Present day...

"KILLIAN." HENRI STOOD and rounded his desk to greet the owner of Tec-Sec Industries as he was shown into Henri's Paris office. They shook hands and Henri asked, "How are Melodie and the baby?"

"Well. Thank you."

Henri wasn't surprised by Killian's succinct reply. Cinnia had summed it up nicely when she had first met the man who was an international security specialist and held the contract for the Sauveterre family's safety. *Did you meet at reticence school? He doesn't care for small talk, does he?*

They had met eight years ago, when Killian had come to Sauveterre International seeking investment capital to expand his global security outfit. Underwriting Killian's ambitions had been one of the first really big risks Henri and Ramon had taken with their father's money after their initial power struggles with the board. A year into watching Killian skyrocket with his business model and suite of military-grade services, they had hired him themselves.

That had been another type of gamble, a move Henri had not made without a great deal of reflection. Ramon operated on gut instinct while Henri was more fact driven. Killian had a good track record, but not a long one.

Ramon had left the final decision to Henri, after making a very good case for the change. "But we both have to believe in this. If you don't like it, we won't do it," his brother had said.

Which had left the massive responsibility for any muck-ups squarely on Henri's shoulders—where the weight still sat. Heavily.

Fortunately, Killian was a brilliant mind hidden behind an impassive face. Nothing escaped him. Aside from the occasional blip of overly exercised caution, they hadn't had one security incident since signing contracts with him.

Not that Henri planned to become complacent as a result, but he felt he and his family were in very good hands. Even marriage and the arrival of his first child hadn't thrown Killian off his focus on business.

"Coffee? Something stronger?" Henri offered.

"I won't be here long," Killian said with a wave of his hand and hitched his pants to sit.

Henri was relieved Killian was so reserved, not trying to bend Henri's ear about the wonders of fatherhood. Henri didn't need to hear what he was missing. Not when he was still stinging over Cinnia's departure for that very reason.

The recollection jabbed like a rapier into his gut, swift and unexpected. She had left him to find the man who would give her the family she craved. Thinking of it sent a reverberation of frustrated agony through him every time he thought of it, so he refused to think of it and quickly pushed aside the temptation to brood today.

He took the chair opposite, distracting himself by getting to business. "You said it wasn't an emergency. I assume it's a price increase?"

"No, although there will be one at the end of the year

to go with a system upgrade. The briefing for that will come through regular channels. No, this is something I thought was best dealt with promptly and face-to-face. One of my guards—I should say, one of the Sauveterre guards—brought me an ethical dilemma." Killian braced his elbows on the chair's arms and steepled his fingers. "In performing regular duties, this guard became aware of a situation that will be of interest to you, but the guard couldn't come to you without compromising the privacy of your sibling."

Henri frowned. "Which one?"

Killian canted his head. "I work for all of you, Henri. I won't betray the trust of one to another. You'd fire me yourself if I did. This guard was reluctant to say anything, but brought it to me because Tec-Sec is charged with protecting the *entire* Sauveterre family. We take that responsibility very seriously."

"Ramon has an illegitimate child somewhere," Henri deduced, and was struck by something he rarely felt, but it was most acute if it happened to involve his brother. Ramon had something he wanted.

He didn't want children, though. He didn't want the responsibility. He had decided that long ago.

Nevertheless, the idea of his brother becoming a father seared his bloodstream with envy so sharp it felt like pure acid.

Then he heard Killian say, "I would take that up with Ramon, wouldn't I?"

Henri's mind blanked as it tried to recalibrate.

There was no humor in Killian's face, no judgment, no emotion whatsoever. He was a master at hiding his feelings, which was one of the reasons Henri liked working with him. Their dealings were always straightforward and unsentimental.

"One of the girls?" he said, hazarding a guess. It was impossible in Trella's case. There had been that one night three months ago, when she'd slipped out in public as Angelique. She'd been photographed kissing a man—a prince, no less—but she had sworn to Henri that's all that had happened.

Gili was tangled up with a prince of her own, had even taken off into the desert overnight with Kasim while they'd all been in Zhamair for Sadiq's wedding. He'd had a message this morning to say that things were back on, but hadn't had a chance to catch up with her about it.

Even if she was back with Kasim, Gili was so cautious he couldn't imagine her failing to take steps to prevent a pregnancy. She would definitely make arrangements to protect her child if she did happen to fall pregnant. Killian wouldn't have to bring it up with Henri. Same went for Trella, for that matter.

Which had to mean…

"You can't mean me," Henri said dismissively. "Cinnia is the only woman I've been with—"

He ran straight into it like he was in one of Ramon's high-performance race cars and hadn't seen the big, red, tightly stacked, rough-edged bricks cemented into a giant wall that had arrived right in front of his nose.

I didn't ask if you wanted to marry me. I asked if you loved me.

And the reason you're asking is because you want to change things between us. I told you I'd never marry you.

He'd been taken aback that morning three months ago, not having seen that conversation coming, either. They were comfortable as they were. He'd grown quietly furious as she had put him on the spot with her "do you love me?"

He *couldn't*. Too much was at stake.

From there, the separation had unfolded like surgery

without anesthetic. He'd endured it with stoicism so he wouldn't betray how much he begrudged her not being content with what they had. That's all he could offer her. She knew that. *He* had to accept it. Why couldn't she?

I would say that things have already changed, but they really haven't. I've always wanted children. You said when I was ready to start a family, you would let me go. Are you going to keep your word?

Of course. He didn't make promises he wouldn't keep.

They had parted with as much civility as possible. Hell, he'd left the flat and come back a week after she was packed and gone. He hadn't looked her up on social media. There was no point. She rarely posted and the last thing he needed was to see whom she was dating in her quest to marry and procreate.

Now he knew she wasn't dating anyone.

Because she was having his child.

It couldn't be true. *Couldn't.* She would have told him. Unless…

The next thought that followed was a screamingly jagged "was it even his?"

Of course it was. It had to be. Killian wouldn't have brought this news to him otherwise and Henri couldn't imagine… Didn't want to imagine… No. Cinnia was highly independent, stubborn to a fault and honest. She would not sneak around having affairs behind his back. When would she have found the time? One way or another, they had shared a bed most nights and while she had been extremely passionate between the sheets, she had never been promiscuous.

No, if she was pregnant, the baby was his.

But how? She knew he didn't want children. On that point he had been blunt, so what the hell had happened?

Had she stopped taking her pill? Was this pregnancy deliberate?

Did she not realize how dangerous that was?

From the moment the responsibility of protecting his family had become his, he had felt as though a Russian roulette gun was pressed to his head. The mere suggestion he had a child on the way slid an extra bullet into one of its chambers. She wouldn't put that on him. Would she?

An excruciating twist of betrayal wrung out the muscle behind his breastbone as he took in that she had disregarded his wishes.

"I see I've given you a lot to think about," Killian said, rising.

"You have." Henri stood, brain exploding. He was coated in a cold sweat beneath his tailored suit. It was all he could do to form civil words as his mind raced to Cinnia and a demand for answers. Somehow he managed to grasp the relevant threads of this conversation and tie them off. "Ensure the guard in question receives a suitable bonus."

"Of course."

"And submit a quote for extending your services to include my growing family." There were times when he recklessly played tennis in the heat and wound up this light-headed, walking through gelatin. He could barely breathe.

"The proposal is being prepared along with a selection of suitable résumés. Are you headed to London? I have staff on standby if you need them. Let me know."

"I'll go straight to her flat, but didn't you put someone on her the minute you learned she was pregnant?" He snapped the words, straining to hold on to his temper, not wanting the pregnancy to be real, but slamming walls of protection into place with reflexive force anyway.

This would be the longest flight of his life. His palms

were clammy, he was so fixated on ensuring the safety of his child. If she was pregnant, he wouldn't breathe easy until he had Cinnia locked behind the Sauveterre vault-like doors.

"I came here the minute I learned," Killian said. "Less than two hours ago. Although I gather the guard has been aware for a few weeks. Preliminary surveillance reveals she's paying one of my competitors to keep the paparazzi at a distance. They're good enough they would notice if someone started watching her, so we're maintaining a distance. She's staying at her mother's, by the way."

Henri nodded and shook Killian's hand.

"*Merci,*" he said distantly. "And one of my siblings knows about this?" He struggled to take in that incredulous piece of the news along with the rest.

"Yes." Killian refused to say which one.

From there, Henri operated like a robot in a sci-fi thriller. *Get to her.* Order the car, text his pilot they were flying to London, climb on the plane, blow through any obstacle without regard.

Wring Ramon's neck. It had to be Ramon. Was he still in touch with that friend of Cinnia's? Cinnia had told him Vera had married last year.

Henri couldn't imagine either of his sisters learning something of this magnitude and keeping it from him. They were far too softhearted to leave him in the dark, knowing how heavily the family's security weighed on him.

But Ramon would have taken the necessary steps to guard her. He wouldn't be satisfied with leaving Cinnia to make her own arrangements.

It was all a jumble and nothing would make sense until Henri saw her. Topmost in his mind would be... *What the hell had she been thinking?*

* * *

Cinnia was tired. Not just tired because she was building two more human bodies with her own, but because today was one thing after another. Nell had been quick to tell her it was because Mercury was in retrograde, when she'd used the phone from the pub where she worked to say that the Wi-Fi was on the blink at the flat.

Perhaps it was true, since Cinnia's new partner running her London office was having phone and network issues. She was forwarding all the office calls and emails to Cinnia today. Cinnia had asked her tech guy to check both, but he was stuck in traffic. Again, thanks to a certain planet traveling backward, *apparently*.

Dorry, bless her, had something going on at school. She was doing most of her learning online these days, accelerating to finish early. She usually sat at the desk in the parlor across the hall, answering the handful of calls Cinnia typically received, allowing Cinnia to concentrate on the piles of work in front of her.

Not today. Nope. Today Dorry was out and their mother was "pitching in." Which meant rather than screen calls and take a message, or look up a price and answer a simple question, she said things like, "Sorry to interrupt, love, but they want to set up a video chat. How do I do that again?"

When her mother knocked for the billionth time, and pushed in without waiting for an invitation, and the phone hadn't even rung this time, Cinnia snapped, "*Mum*. I'm *working*."

"Well, he wasn't going away, was he?"

Cinnia glanced up and the sight of Henri struck her like an asteroid. Like an atomic bomb that had been packed with nuclear energy bottled up by the weeks of being apart from him. Instantly she shattered into a million pieces—

and had to sit there trying not to show it. Her entire body stung with the force.

He was painfully gorgeous. Cutting-edge dark blue suit, a narrow line of ruthless red in his striped tie, clean shaven, tall and trim and larger than life, as always. His intense personality honed in on her with that piercing quality that made her insides twist with joyful reunion.

It was quickly choked off with a quake of abject fear.

She wasn't ready for this.

Because the flutters in her belly were not just the butterflies of excitement he always inspired. They were the movement of his offspring.

She said a word that was *very* unladylike.

"Lovely to see you, too." His mouth curled in something that was the furthest thing from a smile.

"You called him?" she accused her mother, because that's what one did in times of deep stress: attack the people who loved you unconditionally.

She couldn't believe it, though. She'd been so careful to hide her pregnancy, practically living like a shut-in since she had begun to show. In the most uncompromising of terms, she had bribed and cajoled and threatened her family into silence. How had he found out?

"I did not." Her mother chucked up her chin in offense, silver coif trembling. "But it's long past time you did, isn't it? Shall I hold your calls?"

"Oh, thanks, Mum. That would be great." Cinnia rolled her eyes as her mother closed the door, locking Henri into the library with her.

"Trella told you?" She lowered the angle of her laptop screen to see him better over it, but quavered behind it.

"Trella?" His sister's name came out with the weight of grim consideration. "I was wondering which one of them it was. How the hell does my sister—" He held up a hand. "We will come back to that."

"You haven't talked to her?" Oh, damn. *Sorry, Trell.*

Cinnia glanced at her phone, wanting to warn her friend that big brother was on the warpath, but she had to survive his wrath first.

She took in the way he looked like a caged lion, tail flicking and muscles bunched, ready to pounce. They had argued in the past, but he'd never been this angry. He'd never looked at her like this—as though whatever he'd felt for her was completely *gone*.

Their breakup had been agony for her, but it was nothing compared to the raw squirming torment that accosted her under that accusatory glare of his.

"How, um…" Wait. If Trella hadn't told him, did he even know she was pregnant?

She scooched her chair a little tighter to the desk and tugged her lapels over her noticeably more ample breasts, adjusting the angle of her laptop one more inch, hoping to hide what was pressing up against the edge of her desk.

"Why are you here?" she asked shakily.

"You know damned well why I'm here." He planted his hands on the two-hundred-fifty-year-old Chippendale masterpiece that her mother refused to sell. "Stand up."

"You came to school me on my manners?" She pretended she wasn't torn to shreds inside and lifted haughty brows. "Sorry I didn't rush around to greet you like a long-lost relative!"

He made a choked noise.

"Yes, *chérie.* I think there is a certain courtesy concerning relatives that you have grossly overlooked." His hazel-green eyes were stainless steel. Chop-chop, his gaze warned. Prepare to be sliced and diced.

She had known he would be angry, but this was so unfair. Her hand wanted to go protectively to the bump that had sent him away and was now bringing him back, but not with so much as a hint of pleasure at seeing her again.

She had been trying to work up the courage to call him. Her ego had held her back. Pride and ego. Pride because she was still devastated that he had let her go, obviously feeling nothing toward her despite the fact they'd essentially been living together, and ego because she looked ridiculous.

She gathered her courage and stood, bracing to take it on the chin.

He slid his gaze down and jerked, pushing off the desk, clearly taken aback by the small planet that shot straight out of her middle and arrived a full minute before she did in any room she entered.

"Thanks," she said acerbically, but couldn't blame him. While she was a little plumper in the face and chest, she really hadn't gained much weight except in her middle, where she looked like she'd stuffed a sofa cushion under her shirt. The whole sofa, actually, and she was only midway through this pregnancy!

Henri took a long inhale, cheeks hollowing as he stared at her belly with such laser focus she was compelled to block his fierce stare with her hand.

His own hand went into his hair. His nostrils flared as that cutting glance swung up to pierce hers. "Why would you do this?"

He was gray beneath his swarthy skin. Obviously he was shocked.

She had expected this accusation. It was precisely the reason why she had left him and had worked so hard to put in place a means to do this alone. It still went into her like a knife. Nearly two years, *two years* of never asking him for one damned thing except "do you love me?"

"*I* did this to *you*?" she said, barely managing to keep a level tone. Oh, she felt so discarded and misused in that moment, worse even than when he'd shrugged off their breakup. "I suggest you take a hard look at which one of us is carrying three stone of our combined DNA." It was closer to five, but shut up, bathroom scale.

"You were supposed to be taking your pill."

"And I had the flu for a week last fall."

"I used condoms after," he reminded her, stabbing the top of the desk with his finger.

"I thought we were fine, too. What am I? A reproductive scientist? I don't know how it happened! Sometimes when people have sex, they make babies. Super weird that it could happen to us, right? 'Cause we hardly ever had sex."

Every night. All the time. She wanted to have sex with him right now, the bastard, coming in here smelling all yummy with that aftershave that drove her crazy and not having gained an ounce. If anything, he was sculpted into an even harder, sharper version of the man she had lusted after without reserve.

She looked away, hating her cheeks for flushing with awareness and her body for *remembering*.

If her eyes began to tear, she would throw herself through the curtain-cloaked window behind her.

"I never wanted this responsibility!" Henri blurted, like he'd been saving that statement for miles and miles. All his life. "You *knew* that."

"Then you should have kept your pants on," she hissed back at him.

He glared at her like he was furious with her for forever tempting that beast from behind his zipper. Like he resented her and her pregnancy and everything they'd shared.

Well, she was as volatile as any pregnant woman. Probably twice as emotional as the average. Salty tears rushed up to sting her eyes. Her throat closed with emotion and her inner mercury shot up so high it bounced off the inside of her skull.

"Don't feel you have to accept any responsibility today." She rounded the desk and headed for the door. "This is all my fault. You're completely innocent and have no obligation. I am more than capable of parenting without you." She pulled the door inward and waved an arm to invite him to exit. "Fly. Be free."

He folded his arms, such a filthy glare on his face she should have been turned to stone.

"I'm serious," she said, not caring if her mother was in earshot. She'd heard it all and the rest of the house was empty. "I'm one hundred percent ready to do this on my own. As you can see, I've started working here, where Mum and Dorry have agreed to help with child care. The London office is paying for itself and turning a small profit. So is my flat. Nell and her friends are renting it, but I give what I make on that to Mum since I've kicked out all her boarders. This place has been outfitted with a security system—"

"I'm supposed to imagine that my child is safe in a house where strangers—I'm sorry, *potential clients*—are coming and going?"

"You're supposed to imagine that I did not do this on purpose and I am *not* trapping myself a wealthy husband, as you obviously thought when you came storming in here on your high horse. I knew you would think that of me. I *knew*. Why else did I send back all your stupid jewelry? I could have kept it and sold it, you know! That money would be really handy right now, and God knows I earned it, didn't I? But I never asked you for it, Henri. I never asked you for *anything*."

"Calm down," he growled.

"You calm down! I never wanted to be pregnant by accident! I wanted it to be something I did *on purpose*. With the man I *loved*!"

His head went back like she'd clawed at his cheek. Her own emotions were clawing open her chest, leaving her heart exposed, raw and vulnerable. She railed on, protecting herself the only way she could, with mean, nasty words.

"I never asked for anything until that last morning and I would have settled for you telling me you *cared*. I would have settled for you asking me not to *leave*. But you didn't give one solid damn that I wanted to end it. Bye-bye, Cin. Nice having sex with you. Take your pretty payoffs. And all you can think about right now is how hard this is for you? Try hiding this from paparazzi!" She pointed at her massive bump. "Congratulations on being as big an ass as I thought you would be."

"Are you finished?"

"Really?" she cried. "You're going to take that patronizing tone with me? No, I'm not finished! I'm allowed to freak out! While you've spent the last twelve weeks screwing other women and carrying on with your completely unaffected life, I've been overhauling mine. I've been working damned hard so you never have to be inconvenienced by something that *we* did *together*. Say 'Thank you, Cinnia' and get the hell out of my house."

"Well aren't you the great martyr," he scoffed. "Excuse me for not being grateful when I wasn't given a choice in the matter, was I?"

"Oh, you had choices. And you made them. I'm making the same one, which means getting on with *my* life without *you*. Ta-ta," she sang in a jagged, off-key tone. "I have to get back to work now." After bawling her eyes out over this stupid man and his complete lack of regard for her.

"That's very cute. You know I have no choice. Neither do you," he warned, chin low, brows flat and ominous.

That did it. Her heart broke along old lines and her eyes filled up with hot, fat tears.

"Right," she said in a voice that cracked. "Your only choice is to be saddled with a woman you don't want. A gold digger, obviously, who had her eye on your money all along." She couldn't do this. She started to leave the room.

"Don't put words in my mouth." He caught at her arm.

She shook him off and blinked rapidly, but her lashes were matted together and her composure was thinning to the breaking point.

"Don't put babies in my belly."

"I'll confine it to one, trust me."

"Too late!" It came out shrill and loud. She spun to leave again, but quickly found herself halted and turned back to face him.

Through her tears, he was a blur of ashen skin.

"What?"

"Oh, look at me, Henri!" she intoned. "Have you ever been satisfied with only giving me *one* orgasm? Of course, you had to give me *two* babies!" Her fists clenched and she wanted to pound them against him, against the wall of his chest, as if she could break past the invisible wall he presented to hold off everyone.

Including her.

Especially her.

Instead she found herself stumbling across the hall as he dragged her with him. He plonked himself onto the love seat in the parlor and tugged her to sit beside him.

She was shaking so badly she let it happen and sat beside him in stiff silence, trying to hold her threadbare self together.

He sat with his elbows on his thighs and his face pressed into his wide hands.

She reminded herself she'd had weeks to process her pregnancy and the fact it was twins. He'd had, well, she would guess a few hours on the first baby and about ninety seconds on the second.

Oh, she didn't want to feel sorry for him! Maybe the idea of being a father was hard for him, but it didn't change the fact he'd thought awful things about her and hadn't tried *at all* to hang on to what they'd had.

What had they had? she asked herself for the millionth time. Sex. So much sex and yes, a few good laughs and many excellent meals. But while they'd been profoundly intimate physically, on an emotional level he'd held her off in a dozen subtle ways. Two years she had spent banging her head against that reserve of his and yes, she knew things about him like his taste in music and had a handful more facts on his family than the average person did, but he had never let her into his heart.

How many times had she counseled a girlfriend not to let a man own her soul without giving back a piece of his? Dear God, it was easier to give that advice than take it.

She reached for a tissue off the side table and blew her nose, fighting to pull herself together. She hadn't realized how much poison she'd been harboring over all of this. At one point her mother had accused her of punishing Henri by keeping the pregnancy from him and Cinnia had denied it, vehemently.

Just as she had vehemently done her best to annihilate him in every possible way today, holding off on stabbing him with the fact it was twins so she could do maximum damage when his shields were down.

Because she was crushed and she wanted him to join her in her anguish. She wanted to know she *could* hurt him.

Taking a shaky breath, she started to rise.

His hand shot out and he kept her on the sofa.

"I have to use the toilet. It's nonnegotiable."

He released her and she went, then lingered after washing her hands, studying the profile of her body while avoiding her gaze in the mirror.

She had come from a loving, nuclear family. It was what she had always aspired to have for herself and had never been comfortable as Henri's mistress. He had called her his friend and his companion, sometimes even his lover, but the lack of emotional commitment had always stung.

Part of her had wanted to believe Henri did love her deep down, but she had believed Avery had loved her because he *had said the words* and he hadn't. Even her first boyfriend, who had possessed her whole heart, had let her down. So she had tried to hold off giving up too much of herself to Henri. Had tried to stay autonomous and strong.

Still, she had hoped they were moving toward *something*. When she had turned up pregnant, however, she had had to face how superficial their relationship really was. She hadn't been able to stay with him at that point, not if she had any self-respect left.

At the same time, she knew how he would react to a pregnancy. Ties. Short, cold chains and tall, barbed wire fences.

It wouldn't be easy to hold herself apart from him while he tried to do what she knew he would want to do: pull her inside his castle and shut the drawbridge. *That* was why she had held off telling him. She couldn't be dragged back into his life knowing she meant nothing to him.

That was why she had to find the strength to continue resisting him now.

CHAPTER SIX

THE RATTLE OF china made Henri lift his head.

Millicent Whitley—Milly—came in with a tea tray. She set it up on the coffee table before him. The only noise was the sound of the dishes, but she made a statement with the force with which she served him.

He knew that Cinnia had had words with her mother at different times about their relationship and his refusal to offer a ring. Milly had never said a word to him about it, though. She was too wellborn, too possessed of impeccable manners.

Today, however, she brilliantly conveyed that she would love to see him choke to death on his petit four.

"Thanks, Mum," Cinnia said in a subdued tone as she came back.

"Eat one of the sandwiches," Milly said to her, pointing at the stack of crustless triangles as she straightened with the now empty tray, adding as she passed her daughter at the door, "You're behaving like a harridan."

"Gosh, I hope I haven't ruined my chances for a proposal."

Her mother shut the door on that comment and Cinnia made a face.

"How is your health?" Henri asked her, grasping for a lifeline of fact and logic to keep from being blown into the abyss of unknowns circling in his periphery.

Cinnia blew out a breath that lifted her fringe and came to perch next to him. She reached for a sandwich. "No issues. The weight packs on fast, which is expected. I'm not watching calories, but I try to avoid the empty ones. I've started drinking my tea black and I skip things like mayonnaise and sweets."

He nodded, watching her bite into what looked like plain tuna with a slice of tomato between two dry pieces of bread. Her lips looked fuller. Plump and kissable.

"There haven't been other women." His voice came out a shade too low.

She choked, hand going to her mouth before she reached for her tea and took a cautious sip, clearing her throat and flashing him a persecuted look.

"I'm ready to be civilized, but let's agree to be honest, shall we?"

"I had to date, you know I did." If she was offended that he'd accused her of deliberately getting pregnant, he was insulted that she believed he'd slept with all those women—*any* woman—since her. "Our breakup was well documented. I couldn't appear to be carrying a torch, could I? That wouldn't be safe for you." He'd been plagued by concerns regardless, teetering on wishing she would find a man to look out for her while passionately hating the idea.

"Well, you did an excellent job of convincing *me* you weren't carrying one."

He waited for her gaze to come to his, but she kept her attention on the plate she held.

Her features were softer and, if anything, prettier for it. More feminine. She wasn't wearing makeup, her hair was clipped at her nape, but he found her casual elegance as fascinating as ever.

He wanted her, every bit as much as ever.

He pushed to his feet, restlessly moving away from temptation. He was still processing that she was pregnant. His brain was not ready to take in twins and he was still very much reeling from the anger she'd thrown at him.

"There were no other women," he repeated. "I'm not going to say it again."

It was too much of a blow to his ego. He *couldn't* screw other women. She wanted them to throw toxins at one another? Fine. He would love to tell her how much he resented her grip on him. He felt like a cheat merely allowing another woman's hand to rest on his arm. Had he realized that would be a by-product of a long-term, monogamous relationship, he never would have entered into one.

Damn. He wished that was true, but Cinnia had entranced him from the first time he'd seen her. She still did, sitting there cutting a suspicious glare at him from beneath pulled brows. This connection between them was as base as an alpha wolf imprinted by a mate.

He wasn't comfortable being ruled by anything so visceral, but even now, as he was reeling from this life-altering news, part of him was soaring with the knowledge that he now had the perfect excuse to yank her back into his bed.

"As for expecting things of me, you expected me to behave badly and set me up to do so." He pushed his hands into his pockets. "How long did you think you could hide this? I can see if you had a single baby, you might have convinced the press it was someone else's, maybe pretended your infidelity was the reason we broke up. But twins? Of course they'll assume they're mine and go stark raving mad! How did that even happen?" He tried to wrap his brain around it. "Are they identical? Do you know?"

"One placenta," she said with a bemused shrug. "I realize it's like your family has been struck by lightning three times. I'm buying lotto tickets, but I'm told that's not how it works…"

Her joke fell flat.

She had finished her sandwich and was nursing her tea, brow furrowed in contemplation. He always had an urge to kiss that little wrinkle in her brow when she looked like that. She always tsk-tsked at him when he did, complaining it broke her train of thought.

Because he invariably wound up kissing her mouth next, and that led to making love.

That's probably why he liked to kiss her brow.

Could they make love? What the hell was wrong with him that that was all he could think about as he faced such a daunting prospect? Escape, he supposed. Making love with Cinnia had always provided him with a sense of peace to balance the rapid juggling of priorities that was the rest of his life.

She rubbed between her brows with two fingers, like tension sat there.

"I knew I'd have to tell you," she mumbled in a disheartened tone. "I was putting it off because I know what you're going to say, and…" She dropped her hand and said firmly, "I don't want to marry you."

In his lifetime, there were a handful of words that had gone through him like bullets. *Trella's been taken. Your father is gone.* Now, *I don't want to marry you.*

He'd been trying to ignore what she'd said earlier about wanting children with the man she loved. He had been fairly convinced she was in love with him, even though she'd never said the words. Then she had left him.

Today, all that rage she'd aimed at him? His brain told him that came from a scorned heart. He *had* scorned her.

Bye-bye, Cinnia. Yes, he had let her go without a fight. What was he supposed to have done? Denied her the family she had told him from the beginning that she wanted? If she had been telling the truth on her way out the door, and really *had* wanted to run off and find Mr. Right, to make a family with that unknown man, Henri had been honor bound to let her.

She hadn't been telling the truth, though. She'd been *testing* him.

He'd failed, obviously.

Had his rejection killed whatever she *had* felt?

He pinched the bridge of his nose. It didn't matter.

"You still have to do it," he informed her.

"No. I—"

"Cinnia," he interrupted, unequivocal. "I will accommodate your career if you want to keep working. Dorry can be our nanny. I will give you just about anything you ask of me, but you know that you are coming with me today. Our children must be protected. *You know I won't negotiate on this.*"

"No."

Cinnia had never been a pushover, something he had always admired in her, but Henri had written the book on how to get your way. He didn't bother saying anything, only gave her a look that warned she was wasting both their time.

"Divorced people raise children apart. If you want to amp up my security, that's your prerogative, but I'm handling things just fine."

"Are you?" He scratched his cheek and glanced toward the draped window. "Shall I open those curtains and we'll see how well you're keeping the world at bay?"

"Oh, you didn't drag a swarm of those buzzards here, did you?"

He could have taken steps to lose the cameras they'd picked up at the airport, but he'd been too intent on getting here. "You know what my life is like."

"I do!" she asserted with a crack in her voice as the words burst out of her. "And I put up with your guards and all the awful trolls who post those nasty things and I never made a peep because it was my choice to be with you. I could have walked away anytime if I didn't like it. And I did! So don't ask me to sign up for a lifetime of it. Don't try to *make* me."

His fuse, the one that had slowly been burning down since Killian had set a match to it, reached powder.

"Do you honestly think either of us has a choice?" He managed to keep his voice under a roar, but it was fierce with the bitter vehemence he normally kept pent up. "Don't tell me how hard it is to live under such attention. I know, damn you."

She sat back, intimidated by his muted explosion, but he couldn't contain it. Not if she was going to throw it in his face as the reason she didn't want to marry him. Damn it, she *would* understand, if nothing else, that it wasn't just a nuisance, but a life-threatening menace.

"Trella wasn't kidnapped because we're *rich*. We were valuable because we'd been portrayed as a national treasure. *I* didn't sign up for that. None of us did! And did they have the decency to give us privacy after she was rescued? Hell, no! It was worse!"

He thought of all the ugly conjecture that had followed them for years.

"They pushed her into a breakdown and I swear they caused my father's death. He might have withstood nearly losing his child, but trying to keep us out of that microscope? There was no pity for the pressure he was under! If he showed signs of cracking, they turned it higher. *I know.*" He smacked his hand into his chest. "I stepped into his shoes. The corporation is enough for any man and then to be worried sick for the rest of your life that another attempt would be made? All because those vipers insist on making us into demigods?"

He threw an accusatory point at the closed curtain, vainly wishing, yearning, for the ability to incinerate every camera on earth.

"I hate them. I bloody well hate them. They're vile and they set us up to be victimized in every way—by trolls, by opportunists, by criminals who want to steal a child for profit."

He ran his hand down his face, trying not to think of such a thing happening to *his* child. He pointed a railing finger at her.

"You have no idea what they're really capable of. And you definitely don't have the resources to hold them at a decent distance. So, no. Do not think for a minute that I will leave it to you to 'handle' security. I can't even say I will take the babies and let you live your life away from us because you are part of this now, like it or not. So you *will* come to Paris with me and *I* will handle security."

At some point she had pulled a cushion across her chest and had drawn her knees up, buffering herself against his outburst.

He pushed his fingers through his hair, scratching at his tight scalp, feeling like a bully now that the worst of his temper was spent, but—

"This was why I didn't want children. This is how I knew it would be." He was defeated by circumstance. "But we're here now, so we'll do what we must. You'll marry me."

"No," she said in a husk of a voice, lips white.

He drew in a tested breath, frustration returning in a

flood of heat. "Did you hear what I just said? *You can't stay here.*"

"Yes, I heard you. Fine. I'll live behind your iron curtain, but—" She swallowed. "But I won't marry you." Her chin came up in what he knew was her stand-ground face.

His ears buzzed as he sifted through her words. "What do you mean?"

"I mean I'll live with you, but I won't *live* with you." She flushed and pulled her shoulders up defensively around her ears.

"You don't want to sleep with me?" His heart bottomed out. She couldn't mean that.

She flinched and looked away, blinking hard. "No. I don't."

"Liar." It came out of him as a breath of absolute truth. A dying wish.

She made a face that held shame and guilt and self-contempt, but when she brought her gaze back to his, she didn't try to convince him she was being honest. She couldn't.

The naked vulnerability in her expression caught at something inside him, though. It was out of character and gut-wrenching, making him tamp it down with resistance. Cinnia was tough. He had always liked that about her. He needed her to be resilient and as impermeable as he was. It was too much on him if she was fragile.

Despite the revelation of weakness, however, she was resolved.

"We can carry on pretty much as we did before." Her voice was a tangle of conflicted emotions. "I'll work remotely around your schedule and go into my office when I can. I'll have to see what my doctor says about travel, but I'm not up for a lot. I was planning to take a few months off work when the babies come, but I don't care where we are when that happens. We can figure that out as we go along, but I'm not going to take up with you again."

"It's not 'taking up.' It's *marriage*." Did she realize how deeply she was insulting him? "Are you trying to make some kind of point? Damn it, Cinnia, are you still trying to prove something to a man in your past who has nothing to do with me?" He wanted to physically hunt down the jerk and shake him.

Her stare flattened to a tundra wasteland of blue that chilled him to the marrow.

"Do you *want* to marry me, Henri? If I wasn't pregnant, would you even be here right now? If I had ended things purely because I wanted to marry and have children, would you have crossed a street to even say, 'Nice to see you'? No. So, no, I'm not being perverse. Yes, this has everything to do with you. If you want to marry me, you can damn well get down on one knee, ask nicely and *mean it*."

Cinnia went upstairs to pack.

Henri forced himself to sit and drink his cold tea while he ate a sandwich, determined to regain his composure after his flare-up.

He hadn't meant to ignite like that, but Ramon was the only one who really understood how dark that time had been after their father's death. Grief had crippled all of them, but a fresh round of attention had fallen on them with the funeral—the girls especially. At fifteen, they'd been long-legged fillies, striking in their youthful blossom of womanhood, hauntingly beautiful in their sorrow.

He and Ramon were used to being sexually objectified by then, but nothing had prepared any of them for the reprehensible, predatory way strange men had begun stalking the girls once the photos were published. For Trella, it had been particularly insidious, sparking panic attacks that had been debilitating.

While other young men his age were drinking themselves stupid, hooking up and partying, he and Ramon had been forced to a level of maturity that exceeded any geezer on the board.

In some ways, combating those dinosaurs for control of Sauveterre International had been a much-appreciated outlet. Ramon was the verbal one, passionately arguing their case and hotly quitting a tense meeting to let off steam by racing cars.

Henri had retreated to spreadsheets and numbers, facts and figures that fueled his ruthless pushback against attempts to sideline him.

He couldn't count the nights he'd sat in a room lit only by the screen of his laptop, angry with his father for abandoning him to this, but sorry for him. Empathizing with him while silently begging for advice on how best to protect his mother and sisters.

Things had grown easier as the girls had matured and taken more responsibility for their own safety. Hell, Trella's self-imposed seclusion had been a relief when it came to how vigilant they all had to be, not that Henri would have ever asked her to go to those lengths.

But he'd never forgotten those first years of wearing his father's mantle, wondering how he would withstand the next day or the one after that. The pressure was too much to expect of anyone. It had hardened his resolve against ever having children and being charged with their safety.

Yet here he was. With Cinnia.

Leaning on his elbows, he rested his tight lips against his linked fingers, examining the assumption he had made before he'd even confirmed her pregnancy. Of course they would marry. For all his reluctance to become a family man, he was the product of one. He and Cinnia were compatible in many ways. It was a natural conclusion.

But she didn't want to rekindle their physical relationship. If the reason was medical, she would have said, "I can't," but her words had been "I won't."

Because she wanted more than sex?

Do you love me?

He jerked to his feet as though he could escape his own ruminations by physically running from them. Now, more than ever, he couldn't afford such distractions. Look at him, dwelling on things that couldn't be changed when he should be putting wheels into motion for all that *had* changed.

He shook off his introspection, decided to tell his mother when Cinnia was with him, and video-called Ramon.

When he and his brother had been children, his mother had always spoken Spanish while their father had used his native French. They had wanted their boys to be fluent in both. Before he and Ramon went to school and learned otherwise, they had thought that if someone spoke to them in Spanish, they had to reply in French. It had amused Ramon to no end when the girls had come along and done the same thing. They were all still guilty of reverting to the habit in private conversations with each other.

"Cinnia is pregnant," Henri announced in French.

Ramon visibly flinched. "*Es lamentable.* Who is the father?"

"Me. I am the father," Henri said through his teeth, offended his brother would think otherwise. "The babies are mine." He was still assimilating that outlandish fact. Saying it aloud made it real and all the more heart-stopping.

"'Babies?' *Twins?*" Ramon choked out with disbelief. He swore. Let out a laugh, then swore and laughed again. *"Es verdad?"*

"So real." Henri wiped his hand down his face, trying to keep it from melting off. "You and I need to talk. She has four months to go, but they'll probably come early. I'll have to curtail most of my travel this year. We'll station in Paris, but you and I must discuss how we'll restructure. The press will be a nightmare." His knee-jerk response when thinking about their name in the press was to worry about how it affected Trella, which reminded him... "Trella knew. Did she say anything to you?"

"Knew that Cinnia was pregnant? *No dijo nada.*"

"She's still in Paris?"

"*España.* But go easy." Ramon held up his hand in caution. "She's doing so well. Don't give her a setback."

Henri took that with a grain of salt. His sisters often accused him of smothering, but he still tried to head off potential problems before they triggered one of Trella's attacks. Given how agonizing the episodes were for her, he would never forgive himself if he *caused* one.

He didn't bother defending himself to his brother, though. The warning was pure hypocrisy, coming from Ramon. Ramon and Trella had the most volatile relationship among the four of them. Where Angelique was so sensitive she had always cried if her sister said one cross word in her direction, and Henri was so pragmatic and coolheaded he refused to engage when Trella was in a snit, Ramon had always been more than eager to give her a fight if she wanted one.

But Ramon and only Ramon was allowed to get into a yelling match with their baby sister. Somehow it never caused an attack and sometimes, they all suspected, it had been the only way for Trella to release her pent-up frustrations in a way that didn't leave her fetal and shattered.

Nevertheless, Ramon would not stand between Henri and Trella on this.

"There is no good explanation for leaving me in ignorance." If something had happened before he'd been able to set precautions in place... He refused to even consider it. "It was cavalier and reckless."

"I'll speak to her about it," Ramon said.

Henri made a mental note to be in another country when that happened, saying only, "Meet me in Paris. I'm taking Cinnia there as soon as she packs."

He ended the call and tried Trella. After a few rings, she came on the screen shoulder-to-shoulder with Angelique, both of them wearing a look of apprehension.

"I forgot you were home, too, Gili," he said as he recognized the lounge at Sus Brazos. "Is Mama there?"

"Siesta," they said in unison.

He nodded. Seeing them side-by-side like that, he was struck by Trella's very slight weight gain. It allowed him to get a firmer grasp on the temper he was already holding on a tight leash. After the kidnapping, she'd gone through a heavy period. Comfort eating, her therapist had called it. Insulating. The press had labeled her The Fat One and that had been only the tip of the iceberg with the ugly things printed and said about her.

By the time their father had died, her eating habits had gone the other way and she'd been starving herself. They'd worried about how underweight she was and then the panic attacks had arrived, carrying on for years. After a lengthy bout of trying different medications, which had amounted to drug dependency more than once, she had removed herself from the public eye. Eventually her moods had stabilized, then her weight and overall health had, too.

Things had been going so well that, when Sadiq had announced he was marrying last year, Trella had insisted on coming out of isolation to attend his wedding a few weeks ago. The event had forced her back into the public eye and he and his siblings had been walking on eggshells since, holding their breaths in fear she'd backslide.

Henri wanted her to live as normal a life as their family was capable of, but that fullness in her cheeks and the trepidation in her eyes made him worry that she was not coping as well as they all hoped. He was angry, but forced himself to tread gently.

"I'm at Cinnia's mother's," he began.

"I know. Cin texted me."

That was a surprise. He hadn't seen Cinnia fetch her phone. "Am I to understand you knew about this, too, Gili?"

"Not about Cinnia, no. Trella just explained that bit after she got the text that you were there. Congratulations." Her smile grew to such bright warmth and sincere joy he wanted to groan. Leave it to Gili to undermine his bad mood with her soft heart and warm enthusiasm. *"Twins?"* She patted her hands together in a little clap of excitement. "We each get one! *Merci*, Henri!"

He and Ramon had thought the same thing when their mother had produced a pair of girls when they were six, one for each of them. He might have rolled his eyes, but something in what she'd said niggled.

"What do you mean, you didn't know about *Cinnia*? What *did* you know that I don't?"

Angelique looked at their sister.

"Um." Trella's mouth twisted as she bit the corner of her lip. She held Gili's gaze with a pleading one of her own.

Gili put her arm around her, bolstering her. "*Ça va*, Bella. Just tell him."

"Cinnia didn't tell you where we bumped into each other?" Trella asked, catching his gaze in the screen, then flicking hers away.

"Here in London, I presume. You've been coming to see a client the last few weeks, haven't you?"

"Sort of. Cinnia is a client, right? She couldn't buy maternity wear from anyone else without risking a tip-off to the press."

"Bella," he said in his most carefully modulated tone. "I'm trying very hard not to be angry with you, but I have every right to be. Don't make it worse. Whatever you need to tell me, spit it out."

Her eyelashes lifted and she finally looked at him, speaking swiftly and sharply. "We saw each other at the clinic. The prenatal one. I'm pregnant."

He sat back, absorbing that along with the three dependents he'd just picked up—six, actually, because Cinnia's family would be under his protection, as well. Now, his vulnerable, fragile baby sister was…

He closed his eyes, unable to take it in.

"How…?"

"I was blessed by God, *obviously*. Same as Cinnia," Trella said with a bite in her tone. Then she picked at a nail and mumbled, "It wasn't anything bad. I had a chance to be with someone—"

"The prince. The one you were photographed with a few months ago?" His sisters were even more difficult to tell apart than he and Ramon, especially in photos, but he'd known at the first glance that Trella had been the one caught kissing the Prince of Elazar. Since he'd helped her impersonate Gili himself as part of her process of moving in public again, he hadn't been too hard on her for going rogue.

Now, however…

"You didn't even know him."

"I won't confirm or deny until I've figured out what I'm going to do," Trella mumbled.

"Speaking as a man who just missed several weeks of impending fatherhood, *don't do that, Trella*. It's bad form."

"I'm the one who told her to hire guards and I offered to pay if she couldn't. And speaking as a woman facing an unplanned pregnancy, *this isn't about you*. I *will* handle this, Henri. But I have enough on my plate worrying about myself and my baby without bringing the father into the mix. So does Cinnia, by the way, except she has *two* babies to worry about. Plus, you were the idiot who didn't ask her to stay when you had the chance. *That's* why you missed those weeks, so don't throw that on me. Ugh. I have to go to the bathroom." She pushed to her feet.

As Trella stormed off, Gili gave him a sympathetic look. "Pregnant women are moody." She skipped her gaze in the direction Trella had gone. "Don't tell her I said that. But, you know, keep it in mind with Cinnia."

"How is she, really?" he asked.

Gili's brow pulled with worry, but there was a wistful, pained quality to it. "She's trying so hard not to lean on *anyone*, especially me. Obviously it's a lot to deal with, but I think that's why she's refusing to, you know, tell the father. She doesn't want to feel like a burden again. Give her some time, okay?"

"Oh, I have quite enough to keep me busy here. But you'll tell me if she needs me."

"I will," she promised.

"And how are you?" Had it really only been yesterday that she'd sent him that beaming photo of her with Kasim? She had captioned it "this time we're serious."

He expected a joyful response to his question, but she pulled a sad face.

"Kasim had to go back to Zhamair. I won't see him again until the end of the month. But we want to have a little engagement party." Now came the smile and she was incandescent. "That will take a few weeks to organize, given all our schedules, but I'd like to do it here. Now I'm wondering about Cinnia traveling?"

"We'll have to check with her doctor."

"Please do. If we have to go to London, we will, but I'd rather stay here."

"Agreed." They all relaxed at their childhood home in a way they never could anywhere else.

Besides, he anticipated making his home there with Cinnia, at least at first. His mother still lived there, but she would be thrilled to have them while they worked out exactly where they wanted to live and built their own heavily guarded accommodation. She had despaired for years at having no grandchildren and had been fond of Cinnia. She would express only delight when she heard they were reunited and expecting.

He ended his call with Gili and took the tray to the kitchen, checking in with Milly.

"Thanks, love," Cinnia's mother murmured. She was leafing through an old-fashioned telephone book, flipping through the *C* section, he noted as he set the tray on the island across from where she stood.

"If you're looking up churches, don't bother. She said she'll live with me, but refuses to marry me." He skipped the part where she'd refused to "take up" with him—it still stung.

"Mmm. Claims to be the sensible one." *Flip*. "Perverse is what she is. My husband was the same. It's his fault she's like that, too. The mess he left when he died. Same reason, too. Figured he knew better and the government could go hang with their taxes and formalities and such." *Flip*.

"She seems to be doing well for herself, helping people

navigate those regulations and avoid that kind of debt."
He had to defend Cinnia. She worked hard. Surely her
mother saw that.

"Oh, she does. I only mean she has that same streak of
independence my husband had. And his stubborn… She
calls it a failure to plan, but no, it was a kind of anarchy,
his refusal to fall in with what was clearly the accepted
approach. He was being a bit of an ass, trying to prove he
knew better. She's the same, completely determined to
show her dead father the choices he should have made.
And show me that a woman should never rely on a man,"
she added pithily. "The exact same obstinacy channeled in
a different direction. But you're quite right. I'd have been
in the poor house long ago if not for Cinnia knuckling
down with her career and sorting things out for all of us."

Flip.

Henri thought again about how hard life had been after
his father had passed. Their situations were very different, but Cinnia's devotion to her family, her desire to look
out for them, was every bit as strong as his. She must have
been overwhelmed.

"How old was Cinnia when you lost your husband?"

"Fourteen."

"Fourteen," he repeated, wondering why he didn't know
that already. For all the times she'd admonished him as
being reticent, she wasn't terribly forthcoming about herself. "That must have been a lot on you at the time."

"On Cinnia," she amended with dismay. "Little Dorry
was barely walking. I was a wreck. Well, you know. It's
devastating for the whole family when the cornerstone is
gone, but I was completely unprepared. I didn't know how
to even pay a bill. Genuinely didn't know how to write a
check or how to call a plumber if the sink backed up. All
I knew was that I needed to keep my girls in this house.

It's the only home they knew. That's all you think, isn't it?" She set her hand on the open book and looked at him, old grief heavy in her expression. "Hang on to what's left so you can stay on your feet after such a terrible blow."

Henri nodded. She was stating it exactly right. His mother had been shattered, his sisters distraught, he and Ramon overwhelmed.

"Cinnia doubled up with Dorry so we could let her old room along with the rest. It wasn't worth asking the other two to share. You've met them. You know what I mean," she said with an exasperated shake of her head. "The blood wouldn't have come out of the carpets, but at least they express themselves. Not Cinnia. No, she and Dorry bottle everything up and use it like fuel to get where they're going. Heaven help you if you try to give either a leg up. Dorry is allowed to answer the phone because Cinnia pays her to do it. Quid pro quo, but if I so much as pick it up so it stops ringing? Well!"

Henri folded his arms, thinking of the way Cinnia had refused to let him glance over her business plan until after she'd secured financing elsewhere. Then there had been her reluctance to tell him what she was looking for in a flat, let alone the location she preferred or the price range she could afford. As it turned out, living above her office space had been her plan all along, and a sensible one, but he'd been in the dark on the entire thing until she'd closed the deal. It wasn't just that she hadn't wanted his help, he was seeing, but she needed every last shred of credit to be hers. She *was* independent to a fault.

"That self-sufficiency isn't just because of your husband's situation, though, is it? Tell me about that boyfriend she lived with in London."

"Avery? That is a perfect example of how obdurate she can be. She let that, well, it's not fair to call him a ne'er-do-well, but you could tell at first glance he wouldn't amount to much. I made the mistake of saying I thought she could do better and that was it." Her hand went up in surrender. "She let that boy attach to her like a lamprey. I say 'boy' deliberately. Her first suitor wasn't ready to act like a man, but you could see straight away he had some stones. You remind me of him, if you want the truth."

Henri wasn't sure how to take that, especially when Milly was taking his measure with such a shrewd eye. He didn't like talking about Cinnia's past, either. Not when it included men her mother knew so well.

Aside from Cinnia, his mother had rarely met any woman he'd slept with. Cinnia was the only woman he'd ever trusted enough. First he'd taken her to watch Ramon race a few times, then he'd included her in a dinner with Gili in Paris after she began staying with him there. They'd been seeing each other a full year before he'd taken her to Spain for his birthday, where she'd finally met Trella and his mother.

Those had been big steps for him and she hadn't pressed him to meet and mingle with her family, either, disappearing for a dozen lunches and overnights to see them before she'd started inviting him to accompany her.

He'd been relieved, but now it irritated him that other men had come and gone from this kitchen. He'd had many lovers before Cinnia. Why did he care that she'd had *two*?

"James would have been a good match for her, but they met too young. He let her down," Milly continued with a disheartened sigh. "She went to the opposite end of the spectrum with Avery. Saw him as safe, I suppose. Not so capable of breaking her heart."

That was why he hated the thought of her previous lovers. No other women had impacted him the way Cinnia had, but those other men had been fixtures in her life. They'd shaped her. They affected how she reacted to *him*.

"Avery could barely spoon his own oatmeal. It was my fault she got in so deep with him, of course. 'Mum thinks we should marry for money.' I never said that." She held up an admonishing finger, then waved it away. "But that doesn't matter. She had to prove she's a feminist who can support a man, like someone would pin her with a Victoria Cross for *that*. Oh, she wanted so desperately to make me eat my words about him. And how did that turn out? He was a complete waste of her time and stole a thick slice of her savings, didn't he? Exactly as I called it."

She lowered her nose to the book and gave another page a loud flip.

Everything she'd said had given him a fresh view of Cinnia. Not so much a new angle, as a deeper understanding of her edges and shadows. Was this why she was holding him off? He came on strong at the best of times and his children's safety was a red line for him. She *had* to live with him.

He shouldn't have lost his temper, though. That must have scared her.

At the same time, she must also know he wouldn't let her down the way those other men had. He kept his promises.

You said when I was ready to start a family, you would let me go. Are you going to keep your word?

Of course.

The pit of his belly roiled.

"I have my opinions about you, too, Henri," Milly told him without looking up. "Not *all* of you falls short so if my daughter decided to marry you, I would support her decision." Her head came up and her mouth was tight, her brows arched. "Exactly as I will if she refuses."

He was absorbing that statement as she dropped her attention to the book, adjusted her glasses and set a fingernail onto the page.

"There we are. Classifieds. If she's leaving, I can let out the rooms again, can't I?"

CHAPTER SEVEN

CINNIA DIDN'T HAVE much to pack. Her sisters had been through her wardrobe like locusts once she had grown too big to wear most of it. Trella had been incredibly generous, bringing her maternity clothes and refusing to let her pay. Cinnia had given things back as she grew out of them.

She and Trella had been meeting in secret every other week and without her, Cinnia would have fallen apart by now.

Burying herself in work had also helped her cope. She'd busied herself with bringing on her partner who was taking over the payments on her start-up loan. Then there'd been all the arrangements to set up an office here at the house. For hours, sometimes days at a time, she could forget she was sitting on a ticking time bomb.

But she had always known that Henri would have to be told.

And that he would insist on her coming back for safety reasons. She didn't blame him for that, she didn't, especially after he had pulled back the curtain on how he really felt about the press.

She was still shaken by the bitterness he had revealed. And defeated. Her firm intentions to make her own way had buckled not from his show of temper, but from his helpless anguish. She couldn't, absolutely couldn't, make things harder for him. Not in good conscience.

But her life would change irrevocably now. It would have anyway, she supposed. Twins did that to a woman. But things with Henri would be profoundly different this time. She would no longer be his equal.

Not that she'd been his equal in the past, but she had been able to pretend they were traveling in parallel lanes, living their own lives and intersecting when it suited them for the same reason: sex.

Even before she had turned up pregnant, however, she had known she was following more than pacing. She was becoming more emotionally invested than he was, wrapping her life around his. She had hid it from herself as much as him, but the pregnancy had forced her to confront it. She'd had to ask herself, and him, how deeply he was involved.

"Do you love me?" she had asked him that morning in January, making sure to wait until they'd returned to London so she had an escape strategy that didn't involve getting herself to the ferry.

In typical Henri fashion, he had dodged the question with a faintly bored "If you're looking for a proposal—"

"I didn't ask if you wanted to marry me," she had interrupted sharply, hiding that his attitude stung like a scald. "I asked if you loved me."

"And the reason you're asking is because you want to change things between us." He hadn't even looked up from whatever he was reading on his tablet, like this was a tiresome conversation. "I told you I'd never marry you."

She had sat there with her sip of orange juice eating a hole in her stomach.

Her pregnancy had already been weighing on her conscience for two weeks, earning her a few queries from him about why she was so withdrawn and distracted. He'd even set a hand on her forehead at one point, looking concerned when he asked if she was coming down sick again.

She had been heartsick, aware that he would not be happy about the pregnancy, while deep in her soul, she was *so* happy. There was no man whose baby she would want more.

But not like this. Not so he would feel manipulated and forced into marrying her. Not when she might be a little in love while he clearly didn't have any deep feelings on his side.

So, yes, she had set him up to disappoint her. Maybe if she had said "I love you" first, he might have found some tender words of his own. Perhaps they could have progressed amicably toward an arrangement from there.

She hadn't. She had locked her own heart down tight, preparing herself for rejection and yes, even engineering it so she could walk away wounded yet righteous.

"I've always wanted children," she had reminded him, nearly trembling she was holding herself so tightly together as she gave the greatest shake of dice in her life. "You said when I was ready to start a family, you would let me go. Are you going to keep your word?"

"Of course."

Two words. Bam, bam.

Why couldn't he have at least said he was fond of her in that moment? Why hadn't he said he would miss her? Or acted in some small way like he didn't want her to go? He had spent all the time they'd been together making her think he felt something, even if it was just affection. He was terribly protective of her and often expressed admiration at how hard she worked and what she accomplished. Maybe he didn't laugh outright at all her jokes, sometimes he even gave her a look that scolded her for crossing a line, but he invariably smirked. He appreciated her snark, whether it was witty or facetious.

Why else would she feel so much for him if he didn't at least appear to care for her, too? She wasn't a self-destructive idiot.

Was she?

Did he really feel nothing? From the moment he had walked in here, he hadn't betrayed one iota of pleasure in seeing her again. Just anger and resentment.

You want to change things, he had accused her that day.

She hadn't, she really hadn't. Things had changed all by themselves. Cells had split.

Then she and Henri had.

Her eyes welled as she recognized that nothing had changed between then and now. Absence hadn't made his heart grow fonder. He still felt nothing.

Despair accosted her afresh.

Don't be stupid, she told herself as the pressure built behind her eyes and in her throat. She only cried late in the night, when she lay awake in the dark, missing him, curled around their babies, freezing to death because his side of the bed was empty.

During the day, she was pragmatic and confident.

Which had been easy when she'd been convinced she would hold her position and stay right here in this room.

How would she protect her heart if she was living with him again, seeing him every day?

The pressure behind her eyes built as she contemplated how hard this was going to be. Her breaths were already coming in shaky jags of panic.

She told herself to quit being so silly, but her hand pulled a tissue from the box, then kept grabbing a string of them as she felt her world crumbling around her. The agony of not having his love rose, too much for one or two measly tissues. It was a freight train bearing down on her, filling her throat with a wail of agony that she held her breath against releasing.

She didn't want to love him. It was too big, too hard. It hurt too much.

She buried her face in the cloud of tissues, but this swell of emotion wouldn't be stemmed. Her whole body became wracked by anguish. She had tried to keep everything together and was falling apart. Everything was splitting and rending. She gasped for a breath and it was a ragged sob.

"Cinnia."

His voice, so gentle, so tender, was the last straw. How did he do that? How did he sound like he cared when he didn't?

Her heart broke open and she started to buckle forward, knees giving way under a keening moan.

Strong arms caught her, gathering her, muscles flexing as he picked her up, breath rushing out with the effort. She gave his shoulder a knock with her closed fist, hating him for being virile and powerful when she was fat and weak and falling apart.

He laid her on the bed, coming down alongside her, gathering her into his chest and pressing his lips against her brow, murmuring in French.

She tried to stop crying and listen and wound up wailing, "I don't understand you!" She didn't mean because he was speaking French, but because he was being so *nice*.

"I'm telling you not to be afraid, *chérie*. I shouldn't have scared you, saying those things about being a target. You're safe. I promise I will keep you and the babies safe."

He had it all wrong, but she was so shaken to be held by him, so relieved, she surrendered to emotion and let the pain of these weeks without him release.

He continued to stroke her hair and murmur reassurances. She knew he had probably done this with Trella. Henri had spent fifteen years trying to help his sister recover from something that never should have happened. It was no wonder he drew such a thick line around himself and his family, holding everyone else at a distance.

But even though he begrudged Cinnia for daring to get pregnant, here he was, making promises, letting her burrow into his warmth. It was sweet and right and she cried all the harder.

Bastard. How dare he keep this good, generous heart of his out of her reach?

"Shh. Calm yourself, *chérie*."

"I don't think I can do this," she said, feeling pitiful as she admitted it.

He misunderstood her again. "It's not all on you, Cinnia. You can trust me." He rubbed her back and smoothed his lips against her brow. "I'm here now."

"But you don't want to be." That was the crux of the matter.

He held his mouth against her forehead for a long moment, then sighed a warm breath against her hairline.

"You're fair to berate me for that."

She waited, but he didn't say anything else. Despair rose afresh and she started to roll away.

He tightened his arms, keeping her against his warmth.

"It was painful enough that the kidnapping happened," he said in a low voice that sounded like it barely scraped through a dry throat. "It was frightening enough to live with the knowledge that we're not impervious. But then I became the one responsible for standing watch. Of course I will always look after my mother and sisters, but I never wanted to take on a wife and child. A *child*, Cinnia. If you knew what my parents looked like when Trella was missing."

She swallowed, shocked out of her desolation. He never talked about the kidnapping.

"I was in agony. My mother… It was inhuman what they did to her by taking her daughter. And what they did to Trella? I have *never* wanted to bring the potential for more suffering into my life by having children. That sounds cowardly, I know, but I couldn't volunteer for it."

"I'm sorry," she said, wilting in helplessness, voice nothing but a rasp as she realized he would never forgive her.

"Non," he insisted. "You are not sorry. Neither am I. I'm not." He cupped her face, tilting it up so she could see he was sincere. "I am concerned. I will worry about our children for the rest of my life. But I'm not sorry to be their father."

She could hardly see him through her swollen eyes as they filled with tears of tentative hope.

He caressed her cheek with his thumb. "Our children are not something either of us will regret." He tucked his chin to send his gaze down to her belly and very carefully set his hand on the firm, round bump. "These babies are wanted. By both of their parents. *Oui?"*

Being held by him had already warmed her through, but that touch, the reverence in his gentle, splayed hand, sent joyous light through her, so sharp and sweet she had to close her eyes to withstand it. She ducked her head against his collarbone, feeling all the sharp edges of her broken heart shifting, trying to find a way to fit back together.

"Yes." Her lips trembled as she felt his hand move, lightly exploring. It was pure magic.

"How are there two in there, Cinnia? That's unbelievable."

As if they knew it was him and wanted to say hello,

a tiny rolling sensation went through her abdomen. She choked on a little laugh.

"Did you feel that? Maybe it's not strong enough—"

"Shh." He seemed to hold his breath as they both held very still.

Pressure nudged where his hot hand rested. He let out a breath of wonder.

"Is that really them?" he whispered.

"You don't have to whisper. They're not sleeping." She tilted her face to look at him again, unable to hold back her smile. He was too devoted to his siblings to withhold his love from his children. She'd always known that, deep down, but she was still relieved to see him react with the beginning of parental love. She was overjoyed. "It's incredible, isn't it?"

"It is nothing like I imagined it could be." He shifted so her head was pillowed on his shoulder.

She relaxed, comforted by his seeming desire to get to know his babies through the wall of her belly. But she had to ask—with more than a little trepidation. "You really don't hate me for this? I swear I didn't do it on purpose."

A pause, then his voice was very grave, rumbling beneath her ear. "I know. And I could never hate you."

Not "I love you." Not even "I care." Just "I don't hate you."

Fresh despondency closed her eyes, but she had to wonder if he was withholding his heart because he was afraid of being too attached. What if something happened? As he said, he had every reason to believe bad things could happen if he wasn't vigilant.

Oddly, she found herself thinking of his young self, fifteen and worrying about his missing sister. Her arm went across his chest and she tucked her face into his neck, hugging him tight. Saying nothing, but offering be-lated comfort.

"Are you changing your mind, *chérie*?" he asked, snug-gling her closer with hands that cruised in a familiar way. "Would you like to make love?"

She suspected if this silly belly wasn't in the way, she would feel he was aroused. She was growing warm and boneless, feeling him against her like this.

"No," she lied, shifting so her head was on the pillow, putting space between them. "No, I—" She sighed, con-fronted by how difficult it would be, living with him again, resisting not just him, but herself. "No." Just *no*.

She wondered how long she'd be able to keep saying that.

They didn't make it to Paris until late the next day.

Cinnia was subdued, making Henri think of those days leading up to their breakup. He'd churned through those moments of pale silence a few times since, always con-cluding she had been deciding whether she wanted to leave him.

He saw it differently now. She had known she was preg-nant. Along with that weighty knowledge, her body had al-ready been under a lot of demands. The Cinnia he thought of as quite tough and impervious had fallen apart in his arms last night, then crashed for almost three hours.

Her mother had cautioned him to let her sleep, imply-ing Cinnia didn't always take as much care of herself as she should in her condition, which didn't surprise him. She was as driven by ambition as he was. But her tears and exhaustion had thrust an unpleasant sensation upon him. Humbleness.

She had been carrying more than his children. Guilt. Fear that he would hate her. He had been honest when he'd told her he could never hate her, but he couldn't give her the love she sought, either.

To counter some of that disappointment for her, he had stood in the doorway of her sister's bedroom, cutting a deal with Dorry.

"My preference is to make Spain our base," he had said. "My mother will be there, but she will be Abuela. We'll need an au pair. Since you were already planning to nanny for Cinnia, I'd like you to come with us, at least for the short term."

"Really?" Dorry's quizzical eyebrow had gone up behind the round rims of her glasses. "Wouldn't you rather, like, have someone professional? Who knows karate?"

"The babies will have their own bodyguards, *absolument*, but the guards' duties will be protection, not feeding and changing. And Cinnia may be homesick without family nearby. It would be nice to have you there." Cinnia often talked about her mother and sisters in a tone of exasperation, but she loved them to pieces. "We both trust you, and you and I get along well."

"Also, his brother won't try to hook up with you," Cinnia had called sleepily through the cracked door of the darkened room behind him.

Henri had shaken his head, secretly delighted to hear her rallying, but sometimes her remarks were in such poor taste.

Dorry hadn't flinched or laughed. She'd given him her sister's exact deadpan look and said, "Forget it then."

"I take it back," he'd told the girl. "Two sharp Whitley tongues under one roof is too many."

He hadn't meant it. They'd all convened in the dining room for a late dinner, Dorry contemplating a year in Spain. He had also negotiated with her mother to bring in staff to serve as security and run the family mansion as a B and B if she wanted to continue letting rooms, but he promised to find her a flat near them in Spain so she could come and go as it suited her, and see her grandchildren.

Those were the simple details. There were a million more complex ones still to work through, but he found himself unable to catch at any of them as they entered his penthouse, tired from a long day.

They had slept last night in the London flat, arriving very late and using separate rooms, then visited her doctor first thing this morning, ensuring she was safe to travel and transferring her file to a specialist here in Paris—whom they'd briefly met on arrival in the city.

He liked the London flat fine. He and Cinnia had made it a sort of base in the past and had been comfortable there, but family came and went from that residence.

This penthouse was his. With six bedrooms, his family each had a room here, but only stayed occasionally. His mother and sisters typically put themselves up in the secure flat atop the girls' design house, Maison des Jumeaux, while his brother made do with hotels—so he could have a guest if he desired.

Henri preferred these spacious rooms with their modern decor and plethora of conveniences. It was his retreat, a space he had purchased for himself for the private terrace overlooking the Eiffel Tower and the Seine.

Cinnia let out a sigh as they entered, exactly expressing how he felt.

She had always been a pleasant companion, providing a side commentary that made cocktail parties or gala dinners that much easier to endure, but always as relieved as he was to close the door on the world.

She took off her coat and hung it herself like she'd arrived into her own home.

He watched with a twist in his gut, realizing how much

he'd taken her place in his life for granted. He'd been impatient when she had sounded like she wasn't satisfied with their arrangement. He had been. Eminently. You didn't mess with perfection.

He'd been furious with her that morning. He'd not only resisted allowing her to stir things in a different direction, but he'd also let her go to prove to himself he would quickly get past any disappointment at her departure.

He hadn't. Her absence had been eating a hole in him, not least of which because he had no interest in other women. It was the longest stretch in his life he'd been abstinent since discovering what the opposite sex had to offer.

She had her back to him, not even looking pregnant from this angle. She was his ever-alluring Cinnia with her wavy blond hair falling down her narrow back and her lovely round bottom creating an exquisitely feminine hourglass below her wide shoulders. Her supple backside flexed as she kicked off her shoes into the closet.

He wanted her. *Craved* her. Had for months.

Hell. When had he not hungered for her? From the first moment he'd seen her, he'd been captivated.

Now, finally alone with her, the talons of lust were taking a firm hold in him—destructive lust, since the press already knew something was up, forcing a lot of trying detours today. He needed to keep his head, his mind, focused.

He ought to keep his distance, but he moved to stand beside her and toed off his own shoes.

He could smell that familiar, elusive scent of hers. Subtle. She never wore anything overpowering. He always had to get in close to catch the faint hints of rain and roses in her hair, lavender and geranium on her skin.

Her profile was stark, shadows playing deep into the contours of her face, making her look pale and shell-shocked. She stared into the closet like she was searching for a passageway to another world.

"What's wrong?" His arm went out in a reflexive need to catch and hold. He hooked it across the top of her chest, pivoting to draw her back into him.

"Nothing." His action turned her and she lifted her gaze to where they were reflected in the mirror by the door. Her hands came up to hold on to his forearm, but she didn't press him to remove his touch.

He looked at their reflection.

Her brow pleated with accusation before hurt clouded into her sky blue eyes. She lowered her lashes to hide it, but her mouth remained pouted with disappointment.

In him.

He tightened his arm on her.

"I didn't think I had to ask why you wanted to leave, *chérie*. You told me why. You're not allowed to hate me for letting you go when you said it's what you wanted. I'm not a barbarian. I wasn't going to keep you against your will."

Laughter burst out of her. "Really? Where am I now? With how much choice?"

He folded his other arm across her, splaying a hand over the babies he would protect with his life. "You could have been honest. *You* decided to make this hard by not telling me."

Her lips trembled and she tightened her mouth to steady them. "Two years is a long time to be a courtesan, Henri. I wanted to know I meant more to you than sex for hire."

"You do."

"Do I?" Her gaze flashed back to his in the mirror, filled with dejection as she nudged her bottom into his groin. Where he was hard. "That's all you ever gave me. That and jewelry, and now a pair of babies. Never *you*."

"This *is* me," he said through gritted teeth, barely containing himself as a rush of excitement went through him at the press of her soft cheek. He chucked his chin at his reflection. "This man who is obsessed enough to risk bringing you into my home, where you can see the inner workings of my life. Do you honestly think our affair was something I took on lightly? No, damn you, it wasn't. It's a weakness. A dangerous indulgence. But I wanted you. I want you all the time. Do you really expect me to apologize for giving in to that? When you want me every bit as much?"

She tried to glare him down in the mirror, challenging his claim, but he dismissed her bravado with a scoffing breath of a laugh.

"You're nipples are hard, *chérie*. Think I haven't noticed?" He slid his hand to cup her breast, full enough now to make him splay his fingers to contain the abundant flesh.

She gasped and hunched away from his touch, bumping into him to escape the pressure.

He released her with a jolt of shock. "I hurt you?"

"They're really tender." Her eyes were shiny with tears.

He turned her to face him and asked, "*Can* you make love?" The doctor had said it was safe, but if it would be painful for her—

She threw back her head and he braced for another rejection.

But as he held her gaze, unable to disguise how ferociously he ached to make love with her, the glow of outrage dimmed in her eyes.

His pulse hammered in his throat, in his chest, in his groin. He might have tightened his hands on her arms, unconsciously urging her to match his need. He couldn't be the only one affected this deeply. It was too much to bear.

Her blue irises began to swim with longing and her weight pressed into his hold. Her shoulders dropped in capitulation.

He swore, control snapping. He cupped her face and kissed her. He tried to be gentle, tried to hang on to a semblance of control, but damn it, it had been *so long*. He opened his mouth wider to take full possession of hers, finally tasting her again and feasting on what he'd been missing. He curled his fist into the silken tresses that had grazed every inch of his naked skin at one time or another, wrapped his other arm around her so his hand braced between her flexing shoulder blades, and he kissed her without restraint. He took.

Raided.

Owned.

And she gave.

She slid her fingers into his hair and pressed him to kiss her harder, opened her mouth beneath his and met his tongue with hers. She scraped her teeth against his lips and clung across his shoulders with a slender arm and let her knee crook up to his thigh.

She moaned in the way that begged him to take her to bed and find fulfillment with her. Within her.

His skin stung, feeling too tight for the heat of desire exploding in him. It was a monster that wanted to consume both of them. He scraped his teeth down her throat to where her neck joined her shoulder. That fantastic, exciting place that always made her gasp and shiver and soften her knees so she wilted in his embrace.

Mine.

"Henri," she moaned and pushed at him.

Pregnant, he reminded himself dimly, saying, "Bed," as he took a half step back.

"Damn you," she whispered in pained despair. "I need more than sex!"

CHAPTER EIGHT

CINNIA WAS SHOWERED, dressed and putting the final touches on her makeup when Henri knocked and came into her bedroom. He had knocked once, an hour ago, telling her without inflection that he'd let her sleep as long as he could, but that they had a busy day and she should get up.

"Ramon is en route. PR will be tricky. I'll want you in several of my meetings. There will be photos."

He'd been on the phone with someone when she'd slipped into the kitchen for a glass of orange juice and scrambled eggs. She'd stolen a yearning look at his back, admiring the way his white shirt clung across his shoulders and his belted pants outlined his firm butt.

Now she was forced to look him in the eye for the first time since he'd walked away from her last night, stepping onto the terrace and staying there, despite the pecking rain.

She hadn't slept well, having sat on the edge of her bed half the night, fighting the temptation to go to him and damn herself and her stubborn principles all to hell.

Was she just being pigheaded, as her mother sometimes accused? She didn't think so. Henri was an easy man to yield to. To drown in. If she started having sex with him, she would let him take over her entire life—become dependent. She couldn't allow herself to become that weak.

But she suspected he would always be stronger than

her, always, which was unnerving, especially when he strode with that easy, panther-like confidence toward her.

"Yours." He placed an open envelope on the vanity before her.

She recognized it and her heart fell into her toes. It was the courier envelope with her own handwriting. She had stuffed it full of all the jewelry he'd given her and sent it back to him right after their breakup.

His expression was implacable. Confrontational.

There'd been no reaction out of him when she'd done it, which had fed her misery. Now she saw there were very strong feelings on his side, so strong she had to look away, getting the sense he was barely holding back a blast at her that had nothing to do with being rebuffed from her bed.

She twisted her mascara back into its base and set it aside. "Is Ramon here?"

"Any minute."

Damn. Hurry up, Ramon.

She took a half step back from the mirror, gave her hair a flick so it was behind her shoulders and wondered if Henri liked what he saw, then heard her own thoughts and wanted to groan. She wore a blue wrap dress with a satin belt and a tulip cut to the hem. As with any Maison des Jumeaux creation, it was incredibly flattering. Of course, she looked her best.

She still longed for his approval. His hot stare was making her skin sizzle.

"You're not going to see if it's all there?" Henri challenged. "Perhaps accuse me of bringing that in here to persuade you into bed?"

She kept her gaze on her reflection, feeling the sting as her cheeks flooded with color, but refused to let her attention drop to the envelope or even back to what she sensed would be his hardened expression. His voice sounded like granite.

"You said last night that all I ever gave you was sex and jewelry. Jewelry *for* sex, in fact. Whereas I thought we'd settled that argument with this one." He spoke in a tone that held an undercurrent of danger. He plucked out a bracelet, the first thing he'd ever given her, and dropped it onto the vanity with an air of dismissal. Disgust even.

She gave a cry of protest and reached to catch it before it slithered off the edge and onto the floor. Then she stared at the puddled jewels in her palm, inordinately pleased to cradle them again.

She had worn this bracelet almost every day. It was a line of individually set rubies and diamonds. A tennis bracelet, some called it. "Fireworks," he had said of the color in the stones when he'd presented it. "I saw it and thought of our first night."

She had gone through the roof, accusing him of paying her for sex. They'd had a rousing big fight about it. He had been more offended than she was.

"If I wanted to pay for sex, I would have grabbed the first gaudy piece of trash that came along. *Same goes for a woman.* No, I saw something that made me think of the night we met and I wanted you to have it, because I will always remember—"

He had cut himself off and walked away.

Her? Their first time? That night?

Chastened, she had put on the bracelet and had only taken it off to bathe or if she happened to wear something else for an evening.

"Do you know how angry I was when this showed up?" he said now, the steadiness of his tone belying the latent fury within. He tipped the envelope so everything tumbled out.

She flinched and threw out her free hand, keeping everything on the vanity top.

"This—" he snatched up a bejeweled pendant in the shape of a key "—was never, ever about sex and you know it. It was something I wanted you to have."

He had given it to her a few days after she'd closed on her office and flat. They hadn't even made love there until she'd taken possession and she had had the carpets replaced so, no, it absolutely had nothing to do with sex.

"I'm proud of you," he had said as he had pushed the little velvet box across the restaurant table where they were celebrating. "You worked hard to achieve something and did it. Hell, you're walking around sparkling with such pride in yourself, I thought you should have something sparkly to commemorate it."

She'd been bemused yet touched, and had often worn the pendant when she happened to be having a rough time with a work file or even just a gray day. It never failed to pick her up and make her feel good about who she was and how far she'd come.

"This?" He held up an anklet from their first trip to New York. "What sex was I paying for with this?"

She pinched her mouth shut, knowing full well it had been a silly joke between them. She had bemoaned the fact that the Americans seemed to have a fixation with shoes, but she had no interest in which designer was which. He'd given her that cord of gold, the reticulated links heavy on her skin and always a more pleasant conversation piece when the shoe topic came up. She had threatened to get herself a charm of the Statue of Liberty to hang off it, which had earned her such a stare of revulsion, she still snickered thinking of it.

"I enjoyed having you with me in New York. That's all

I was saying when I gave this to you," he said, shaking the little snake of gold.

"Don't," she muttered, worried he would kink a link. She stole it from him and closed it in her fist against her heart.

"What do you care what happens to it? This is a pile of junk, isn't it?" He gave a solid platinum arm cuff a disdainful bat with his fingertips. "It's not like each one represents a special memory between us. It's not like I spent any time choosing these things specifically for *you*. You're right. They're meaningless and I should have thrown the works in the garbage when they came back. I'll do that now."

"Don't you dare!" she cried, knocking his hands away from sweeping everything back into the envelope. "You made me feel lousy, acting like you didn't give a damn that I was leaving, so I tried to do the same to you. All right?"

She pushed herself between him and the trove of emeralds and diamonds, gold and platinum.

"Message received. Our two years together weren't even worth remembering. When that came back, I wanted to—" In her periphery, she saw his fists clench, but his jaw pulsed. His brow flinched. "We had more than sex." His voice was raw, the words bit out between clenched teeth.

Funny thing about trying to hurt someone you cared about. It wasn't nearly as satisfying as you thought it would be.

She dared a glance up into his face, fearing she'd see anger or resentment. There was only regret. Apology, even.

"Is that why you're refusing to marry me? We're good together, Cinnia. Not just there." He pointed at the bed where she had tossed and turned. *"Everywhere."*

She waited, but he didn't profess undying love.

She looked away, blinking at the sting in her eyes. It wasn't so much disappointment as a feeling of inevitability. What would it even prove if he did say the words? She wouldn't believe him.

A painful jolt went through her, realization striking like a hard pulse of electricity, making her catch her breath. She hadn't just been testing him when she'd left. She'd been driving him away, *afraid* to want his love. Proving to herself she didn't need it.

She was still holding him off to protect herself.

"I care about you. *Ça va?*" He ground out the words like he begrudged even giving her that much.

"No," she said, voice strained, facing something she had barely peered into that day in January. She threw back her head, ignoring the dampness on her lashes as she stared into his wary expression. "It's not okay. Because even if you'd said the words that day…"

Her voice thinned and her throat strained to swallow.

"I've heard them before and it didn't matter. I still wound up hurt and on my own. So yes, I knew deep down that you meant these as signs of affection…" She waved at the jewelry. "But I expected to be left to fend for myself eventually. And was."

"That won't happen again," he vowed fiercely. "It's different."

"Is it? I won't take any chances, will I?"

He started to argue further, but they both heard the door chime.

He swore. "That's Ramon."

"I'll be out in a moment," she promised and turned away to fix her makeup.

Henri ruminated as he watched his brother greet Cinnia. Ramon genuinely liked her, probably because she expected even less from him than she had ever demanded of Henri.

Henri disguised a wince, thinking of what she'd said

moments ago. He supposed he should be relieved that she'd essentially told him she didn't want his declaration of love, since she wouldn't believe him anyway, but it was as much a slap in the face as her return of his jewelry.

He couldn't believe she had so little faith in him.

She was pale and Henri imagined that if his brother noticed, he put it down to her delicate condition.

Ramon, however, being an inveterate flirt, still went out of his way to charm her.

In a moment of shaken confidence, Henri watched closely for her reaction. Cinnia tended to respond with smiles of amused tolerance when his brother turned on the charisma, occasionally flattered, but never swayed, never tempted.

He'd seen it the first day they met, of course, but her preference for him hadn't been fully cemented in his mind until the first time he'd taken her to watch his brother race in Nürburg. It had been a good trip, the first one where he introduced her to perhaps not the family's *inner* circle, but people in their regular social circle. She had fit in well. They had all enjoyed the race day and danced the night away afterward.

The next morning, Henri had taken her down to breakfast only to receive a call as they were entering the restaurant. She had gone ahead to the table with Sadiq and some others from their group. While Henri had watched from afar, Ramon had arrived.

Of course Ramon was wearing the same shirt Henri already wore and of course Ramon had tried to trick Cinnia into believing he was Henri.

Henri's hand had tightened on his phone and he'd missed what his executive was telling him as he watched Ramon come up behind Cinnia and set a familiar hand on her shoulder *exactly* as Henri might have done. Without a doubt, Ramon had said something like "*Je m'excuse, chérie.* I'm here now."

Then his bastard brother had leaned down to kiss her in greeting, exactly as Henri would have done.

Cinnia had paused in midconversation, lifted her mouth in absent acceptance of his arrival and kiss—and had nearly leaped out of her chair before Ramon's lips touched hers. Henri had heard her scream of surprise through the window. If Ramon hadn't caught her and kept her on her feet, she would have stumbled to the floor.

Henri might have found it as funny as everyone else if he hadn't been worried she had hurt herself. He'd cut short his call and hurried into the restaurant, where Cinnia, being a good sport, was laughing at herself even as she scolded Ramon to never *ever* do that to her again.

Henri had then heard every account from every other person who had witnessed it, all ringing with great humor and awe that she could tell the brothers apart so easily. Most of them had also presumed Ramon had been Henri. Pretty much the entire party had been taken in by his joke *except* Cinnia.

Cinnia didn't react to Ramon the way she reacted to him.

He might have been reassured by that, but her heart, he was realizing, was as out of reach as his own. It made him jealous of the rapport Ramon still had with her.

"If you laugh..." Cinnia warned with a sideways look.

"I said you look stunning. As always." Ramon held Cinnia's hands out at her sides. His mouth twitched as he took in her belly.

"I look like a boa constrictor after it swallowed a goat."

"Two. Let's be honest," Ramon said, then he laughed as he dodged her attempt to slug his belly. "Small ones. Kids!" He gathered her into a gentle bear hug and kissed her hair, exactly as he would do if he'd teased one of their sisters into reacting.

"You're a brat!" She playfully shoved out of his arms.

Henri was forced to turn away as the doorman rang to announce their second guest. "*Oui*, send her up."

"Who else is coming?" Cinnia asked as Ramon dropped his hand from her arm and frowned a similar inquiry.

"Isidora Garcia." He didn't bother moving away from the door since she would be knocking momentarily. "You would have met her father, Bernardo, at my mother's birthday."

"Oh, yes! He's lovely."

"He doesn't retire until next month." Ramon's scowl held more than confusion. "We have a team of people under him. I thought we agreed to promote Etienne."

"We have a lot of sensitive information to manage. Angelique and Kasim will go public with their engagement in a few months and you spoke with Bella?"

"I did." His brother's mouth flattened and he shot a look at Cinnia. "Do *you* know who the father is? Is it that Prince of Elazar?"

"She wanted me to have plausible deniability," Cinnia told him with a rueful moue. "She refused to say."

Ramon made a noise of dismay. "Regardless, I don't see why you think we need—"

The knock on the door interrupted him.

Henri opened it and greeted Isidora.

She was a Spanish beauty with a fiery hint of auburn in her long dark hair. Her warm brown eyes were framed in thick, sooty lashes. She took after her notorious socialite mother far more than the short, barrel-chested man she called Papa. Henri privately had his doubts that Bernardo *was* her father, biologically, but had never asked. Bernardo had always guarded the Sauveterre family secrets so diligently, he allowed the man his own.

"*Bonjour*, Isidora. Thank you for coming."

"Of course. It's always lovely to see you." They exchanged cheek kisses. Hers were well-defined and aristocratic, perfumed and soft. She turned to greet Cinnia.

Her smile fell away as she saw Ramon.

"Ramon," she greeted flatly.

Isidora was a little younger than their sisters. Given her father's close relationship with their own, and Trella's homeschooling after the kidnapping, at times Isidora had been one of the few playmates the girls had had. The adoring crush she had developed on Ramon through her adolescence had been awkward, but they had never teased her over it. She was too nice. And Ramon had never encouraged her. She'd been too young, for starters, and he was too conscious of her father's protectiveness of her virtue.

As she had grown into womanhood, however, and developed curves that didn't quit, Henri had thought his brother might be tempted. Now, seeing the frost Isidora directed toward Ramon, Henri had to wonder if his twin had finally raced those curves and left a trail of dust.

He introduced her to Cinnia, adding, "I was just explaining to Cinnia that your father has always been a trusted leader of our team. He's more than entitled to enjoy his golden years, but we are very disappointed to lose him, especially since our lives have become very complicated. We need a delicate touch."

"So Papa said," Isidora murmured. "I don't mean he gave me details," she clarified quickly. "Only said he would feel better if it was me, which I took to mean sensitive information." Her gaze flicked to Cinnia's belly.

"He put the thumbscrews to you?" Henri asked, making a mental note to double Bernardo's retirement bonus for coaxing Isidora to take them on. "I've always said we would hire you when you completed your degree," he reminded her.

"I'm only finishing now. That's why I was in London. And I have never wanted to ride Papa's coattails. You know that." She flashed a glance at Ramon. Didn't want to ride with *him*, she seemed to imply.

"I've been badgering Isidora to join our team since she decided to follow her father into PR," Henri told Cinnia. "She would rather work her way up the ranks of an independent career. Does she remind you of anyone?"

"Look at that. I have a twin myself." She smiled at Isidora. "Would you like something? I was about to make tea."

"I'll help you." Isidora allowed Henri to take her coat before she disappeared into the kitchen with Cinnia. He had the impression she was distancing herself from Ramon.

He threw his brother an admonishing look. "You slept with her?"

"I was turned down," Ramon said blithely, but it didn't sound like the whole story—which surprised Henri. The two of them kept little from each other.

"That happens?" Henri asked drily, allowing his brother his privacy.

"I was shocked, too." Ramon threw off his suit jacket as if he was too warm, leaving it draped across the back of the sofa. Business shirts were all the same, especially white ones, but Ramon's wore the exact crest that embroidered the pocket of Henri's. His pants were an identical shade of gray and even his belt was the same.

Henri didn't even bother remarking on it, only asked, "Is it going to affect her work? Tell me now. We need someone in our midst for months. Not Etienne. He's good on the professional side, but with this much personal information…"

"*Sí*, I know." Ramon shook his head in exasperation. "How am I the only one not causing a stir in the press right now?"

"Meaning you won't be working directly with her. Is that your only reason for hesitating? Because she has always shown excellent potential. We saw it when she was a teenager." She'd begun coming to the office on Take Your Daughter to Work days, drafting soft press releases that had shown better composition than finished work turned out by some of their long-standing professionals. "She's as discreet as they come. Learned that at her papa's knee, I imagine."

"There are other reasons she keeps her own counsel," Ramon said cryptically. "But, *sí*, you are right. She's a good fit. She can't stand me, but she's fond of Gili and Bella. They will be far more comfortable with her than anyone else. Cinnia already likes her." He nodded at where the women's laughter drifted from the kitchen.

Henri nodded, satisfied, but caught the look of inquisition his brother sent him.

"*Qu'est-ce que c'est?*" Henri prompted, even though he knew where Ramon's thoughts had gone.

"I thought we signed a blood oath not to have children." Ramon was a master at affecting a light attitude, but he was far from as shallow as he pretended. His voice was dry, but his expression grave.

"This isn't entrapment." Henri grimaced. "It's an old-fashioned slipup. She left because she was trying to spare me."

Ramon dismissed that with a wave of his hand. "*Pah.* It doesn't matter if you didn't ask for the responsibility. We would never leave one of our own at risk. She must have known you would step up."

"Oui." But given how much he now had at stake, he wouldn't have gone after her without the pregnancy as incentive.

The knowledge caused a white light to shoot through him, jagged as lightning, rending something in him. What if she hadn't been pregnant? What if he really had spent the rest of his life without her?

Ramon slapped his shoulder, yanking him back from staring into a bleak void.

"I have your back, *hermano*. Together we'll keep *tus niños* safe. Your wife is my wife."

"A comforting sentiment," Henri said with a humorless snort. "If she was willing to marry me. She's not."

"That happens?" Ramon stepped back, astonished.

"Apparently."

Do you love me?

Did it matter?

Given all he faced, he couldn't allow himself to be preoccupied with courtship. It was better that she was holding him off.

Still, as the women came back and Cinnia's smile of good humor fell away, he found himself snaring her gaze and holding it, searching for something he couldn't name.

"I was just telling Isidora that I don't even want to *think* about a wedding dress until I've got my figure back," she said, expression neutral.

The singed edges of his ego continued to smolder, filling his throat with an acrid aftertaste.

The media circus was in full swing by the end of the month.

They had released a photograph with their statement that they were delighted to announce the upcoming birth of twins, but that wasn't enough. The paparazzi went berserk. Cinnia only went out a handful of times, once for a checkup with her new doctor and twice to visit Henri's sisters at the design house. She was mobbed every time. Her guards earned their exorbitant paychecks, practically needing a whip and a chair to keep the lions at bay.

What made her groan loudest, however, was how many of the photographers didn't even bother capturing her face. Shots of her belly cluttered every gossip rag as if the twins she carried were visible if you looked hard enough. It could have been any woman's swollen abdomen. She told Henri she was going to start wearing T-shirts with obscene logos and vulgar catchphrases.

He gave her his don't-you-dare look, but then suggested something decidedly unprintable, making her snort.

Henri, who rarely spoke to the press unless it was through a prepared statement that invariably pertained to the business of Sauveterre International, became old news. Why photograph any of the adult Sauveterre twins when they could harangue the mother of the newest set? Even Ramon's best efforts to draw fire with his racing antics and half-naked supermodels failed.

Henri would have taken the attention off her if he could. They were living in an armed truce, managing to be civil and, in some ways, falling into their old routine very easily. Most days he worked at his Paris office while she worked out of his home office at the flat, exactly as she used to when staying with him here in Paris. Their evenings were filled with arrangements for their future: how they would modify the family home in Spain to accommodate the twins, signing up for a private birthing class, reviewing résumés for the babies' security staff.

He took pains to include her in all of it, but she felt the undercurrents of being one more thing he had to manage. Maybe some of that was sexual tension, since they were still sleeping separately, but she saw how frustrated he was with the press and precautions and the sheer volume of to-dos.

It fueled her sense that things were tenuous between them, making her all the more determined to maintain her own income and have a fallback position. Which made *him* say she was working too hard, forcing *her* to point out they had enough topics to debate without throwing her career into the mix.

He began swearing yet again as their car was swarmed when they arrived at a hotel in Milan.

Already prickly and nervous, she flinched at his tone.

"You told me the day we met that you've learned to pick your battles," she reminded him, forcing herself to bite back a reflexive apology. It wasn't her fault she was pregnant. She told herself that every day.

"You should be able to move in public without being harassed," he growled as he helped her from the car and held her arm up the red carpet.

She wore sunglasses, but was still terrified the flashes were going to blind her into stumbling. She clung to Henri's arm as she walked. At twenty-four weeks, she was already ungainly, and tonight she'd put on proper heels, wanting one thing to feel normal after so many changes.

They were attending a charity gala put on by a banking family he worked with regularly. Ramon had taken on all the long-distance travel, but Henri was still covering Europe.

She had vainly hoped this weekend would be a break from the paparazzi. She was due for a night out at the very least, even if it was only a business appearance.

It was decidedly more peaceful inside, thank goodness. The hotel was one of the most exclusive in Europe, the guest list for this ten-thousand-euro-per-plate dinner tightly vetted.

Henri guided her through a grand lobby inspired by a fourteenth century Venetian palace. Marble columns rose like massive sentries above them. The wide staircase spilled a line of royal red carpet down its center. Above, crystal chandeliers sparkled and threw glints of burnished light off the gold leaf accents.

Strangers, all dressed in tuxedos and evening gowns, turned to smile at them.

Cinnia had learned to keep a serene smile on her face and keep moving.

They arrived at the coat check and she let Henri take her sunglasses along with her light full-length jacket. It was faintly medieval in its generous cut and flared sleeves. The gray fabric was shot with threads of silver detailing by Trella's clever hand. Her gown was Angelique's finest work, a Grecian style with a halter bodice and an empire waist. The miles of gathered white silk could drape her growing form with elegance through the rest of her pregnancy.

She wanted to believe she looked attractive, but it was hard when her body was so different and the man at her side had grown even more contained as their relationship solidified behind lines of abstinence.

Maybe she should have sex with him, if only to feel close to him again. Of course, her sexual confidence was eroding as quickly as her waistline was expanding. It didn't help that he was acting like he was escorting his sister. He was solicitous, ensured she had a drink, held her chair when they sat for the dinner, but it wasn't the way it used to be. His touch on her was light and incidental, not carrying the possessive, proprietary weight of the past. No stolen caresses or tender brushes of his lips against a bare shoulder.

After dinner, they made the rounds, spoke with their

hosts, Paolo and Lauren Donatelli, along with Paolo's cousin Vito and his new wife, Gwyn. Cinnia had met them a handful of times in the past and they warmly congratulated her.

The music started and Henri asked her to dance.

In the past, she would have slid naturally into the space against his ruffled tuxedo shirt and tucked her hair beneath his chin, enjoying the light foreplay of moving against him.

Tonight they had to angle their bodies to accommodate her bump. She gave a wistful sigh.

"These events are tiresome, I know, but I'd forgotten how much more bearable they are when you're with me." His thumb caressed where his hand was splayed against her rib cage.

He found an extravagant evening like this "tiresome"? Her mouth twitched as she recalled him telling her the first night they met, *This is how I live.* At the same time, she couldn't help softening toward him, flushing with sweetness at his saying he liked having her at his side.

"I should have taken you on a proper date before this, but things have been…"

"I know." She looked up at him, rueful, startled to find his gaze on her mouth. Her foot slipped.

He caught her close with strong arms. Her hip brushed his fly.

Hard?

Her eyes widened and a flood of sensual heat went through her.

He guided them back into the waltz, but there was a flash of something dangerous in his gaze. "Don't look surprised. You know your effect on me," he said in a quiet rasp.

"It's hard to feel desirable when you're pregnant," she mumbled, blushing with self-conscious pleasure.

"Is *that* why you're still holding me off? Because you have nothing to worry about. You're sexier than ever. It's all I can do to behave like a gentleman."

She would have stumbled again if she hadn't been clinging to his shoulders. His hands firmed on her and stayed that way, deliciously possessive. The rest of the dance became as subtly erotic as any they'd ever shared.

She floated in a sea of possibility after that, deeply tempted. As she freshened her lipstick in the powder room, she gave herself a stern lecture about keeping her head and not succumbing to his charms.

But, oh, it would feel so good.

Then she made the mistake of checking her email and her heart stuttered. She had become enough of a liability to turn him off completely.

Who is Avery Benson? Isidora asked. *He just sold a story claiming you went after his money in the past. We should refute his accusation that your pregnancy is a deliberate ploy to snare a piece of the Sauveterre wealth.*

Suddenly the sideways looks she'd been receiving all evening were explained—and intolerable. Cinnia felt sick. Of course people would speculate, but to have it stated like that, by *Avery*...

She turned her ankle returning to the ballroom, having to catch herself on the back of a nearby chair, which only added to the humiliation as people turned their heads to stare even harder.

Yes, I'm drunk along with being a gold digger, she wanted to lash out.

Henri was watching for her and rushed to meet her. "Are you all right?"

"I have a headache." Her throat was so tight, words barely fought their way through it. "Can we go?"

"Of course." He waited until they were in the back of

the car, then said sharply, "You're white as a ghost. Should we go to the hospital?"

"No. Read your email." Isidora had sent it to both of them. There was no use trying to hide from this degradation. She stared out the side window, the darkened Milan streets a blur through her tear-filled eyes.

Henri said nothing, but she heard a couple of taps and a phone call being placed.

"Avery Benson," he requested.

She swung her head around. "How do you have his number?"

Henri covered her hand on the seat between them and squeezed a signal for quiet. "I don't care if he's having tea with the queen. Tell him it's Henri Sauveterre."

"Don't make it worse." Cinnia reached for his phone.

Henri fended her off, giving her a dark glower. "No, this is not a joke," he told his caller. "Retract your story."

"He won't," Cinnia warned.

"No, *you* listen," Henri said in a voice that made her sit back and hold very still.

She hadn't thought he could sound more deadly than he had the day he had railed about paparazzi. He could. He definitely could. Ice formed somewhere between her heart and her stomach, deep against her spine.

"You were on my watch list and have now been elevated to my red list. I take the security of my family *very* seriously—why were you on my watch list? Because you're a known opportunist who can't be trusted. I had a dossier prepared with your contact details for just this possibility. If you had remained in the background, I wouldn't have given you another thought, but now you've shown yourself willing to profit off my family. That makes you a threat so I must neutralize. No, I don't intend to kill you!"

Henri cast her an impatient look.

"I wouldn't call you to warn you, would I? You would be at the bottom of the ocean with an explanation for your disappearance concocted. No, I prefer you alive to see how I dismantle everything you've acquired after Cinnia gave you a leg up... Oh, she did. You had her convince your parents to sell and stole half her savings on your way out the door. Now if you value your house and your job, you will retract your story and never speak of us again."

Henri paused briefly, then sighed.

"Say you were drunk, on drugs, owed gambling debts. I don't care *how* you explain it, just retract it. Prove to me you are not intending harm to my family or I will push you to my blacklist and I can assure you, your prospects for a promotion, or refinancing your mortgage, or for buying that boat you're looking at, will evaporate. I will sue you into obscurity. Cinnia is not a tool you can use. Ever. Not even just this once."

Henri listened again.

"You will not do that. I've just explained what it means to be on my blacklist and that's where I'll put you if you do anything but retract your story. No, she didn't put me up to this. You poked the bear. This is the consequence. Be smart or lose everything."

Henri ended the call.

"I can fight my own battles," Cinnia muttered, mortified.

Henri kept his gaze on his phone as he tapped out a text. "I'll have Isidora help him. He really does need to be spoon-fed, doesn't he? What did you ever see in him?"

Cheeks stinging, Cinnia looked out the side window again, listening to his phone ping a few times with an exchange of messages, presumably with Isidora.

"Hmm?" Henri prompted a moment later. "I'm curious.

What drew you to such a weak man? You're far too smart to be taken advantage of. Why did you let him use you?"

She shifted, uncomfortable. "You didn't have to be such a sledgehammer. We could have talked first and I could have called him."

"You want to *protect* him?" Henri asked, astounded.

"No. But you didn't even… *I can fight my own battles*," she repeated.

"This isn't your battle. It's ours."

"It was about me. He wasn't really intending—"

"Do not ever be naive about people's intentions, Cinnia," he interrupted, sharp and severe. "Promise me that. Trusting someone who seems harmless is a mistake."

Like a math tutor.

She swallowed and nodded. "Fine. But you could have let me do it. You didn't have to make it seem like I was…"

"What?" he prompted.

"I don't know. Not capable or something."

Henri swore under his breath. "This is about your precious independence? You know, when Trella was four, she went through an annoying phase where she wouldn't let me tie her shoes or zip her jacket. You don't have to do every single thing yourself."

"Name calling isn't any more mature than toddler level, you know."

"Did you *want* to talk to him? Because I don't understand what we're fighting about."

"Do you rely on me for anything?" she demanded as she swung around, thinking maybe, just maybe, if she thought she fulfilled some corner of his life that was more than arm candy at a banquet, they had a chance. "Beyond sex and, you know, building two babies you didn't ask for?"

"Pleasant companionship?" he suggested.

"I loved my first boyfriend, you know." She threw it

at him and should have been more pleased at the way he stiffened as it struck, but she just felt raw. "Maybe it was puppy love, but James felt the same. I knew better than to let a man hold too much sway over my life, though. Learned that from losing Dad, right? So I didn't change my plans and follow James to the school he preferred. I followed my own path, thought we could weather it, but he cheated on me and it felt *awful*."

"Your mother said she thought you picked Avery because he was safe. Is that what she meant?"

"Yes." She shrugged off how self-delusional it had been. "He was nice, but socially awkward and, yes, he was the beta in the relationship. Okay? It felt good to be the one in control. To feel adored without risking too much. *You know how great that feels.*"

They held a locked stare. His jaw was granite, shadows flicking in his face as the angle of lighting changed. The car was pulling into the underground parking of the hotel where they were staying.

"Maybe I unconsciously thought if I took care of him, he wouldn't cheat or leave," Cinnia muttered, gathering her purse and straightening in preparation for the dash to the elevator. "Even if he did, it wouldn't hurt like it had with James, but Avery still found a way to make me feel horrible for believing he cared and, yes, that left me convinced I need to do things myself. I hate needing a man for *anything*. Thank you, Guy," she said as the door beside her opened and the guard offered his hand.

She even needed a man's help crawling from a car these days. It was pathetic.

Oscar already had the elevator open. Cameras flashed from between the shrubs outside the open grill windows as they scurried the short distance into the lift.

They didn't speak again until they were inside their

suite at the top of the building. The space was full of plush furniture in burnt reds and toasted golds, welcoming with fresh flowers and bowls of fruit. None of it softened her mood.

Henri took her coat to hang it and she went to the sofa, sitting to remove the stupid shoes that were killing her feet. That's when she remembered she'd had to ask him to buckle them for her earlier.

She let out a muted scream of frustration and dropped onto her side, burying her face in a tasseled pillow. It was that or break down altogether.

Warm hands gathered her ankles and he lifted her feet out of the way to sit, then set her shoes in his lap and worked on a buckle.

"I hate being weak," she said, shifting the pillow so it covered her ear and she spoke from beneath it, arm curled to hold it in place. "I hate that I can't get through a day without a nap. I hate that I can't sit long enough to get through all the work that needs to be done so I can put away the money that you keep telling me I don't need. I hate that you're taking over my bills and won't let me pay for groceries. I hate that no matter how hard I try, I'm becoming dependent on you."

He dropped her shoes away and kept her bare feet in his lap, rubbing them. It felt wonderful and tender and it was one more way she was letting him do something for her. Her breath caught, nearly becoming a sob.

"I hate that those men hurt you and you don't trust me as a result," he said gravely. "You're right that I crave control even more than you do. At your expense, even. I wasn't trying to make you feel weak when I called him, though. I was reacting." He squeezed her feet, warming them. "I would have preferred to kill him, if you want the truth. Apparently there are laws."

He was trying to make light, but she had heard his tone in the car and heard that same ruthlessness now.

"I used to find it so refreshing that you were self-sufficient. Lately, I find it insulting. You *can* entrust yourself to me, Cinnia. I know that's not easy for you, I understand why you're so reluctant, but I have already put many things in place that will ensure you never want. You'll always be comfortable and, to the extent I can manage it, safe from harm. We are a team where these babies are concerned. It's basic parenting dynamics that I do the providing and protecting so you can do the birthing and nurturing."

"If that's you trying to get out of nappy duty already..."

"And she rallies," he said with a warm stroke of his hand up her calf. "You are never weak, *chérie*. It is the last word I would use to describe you. All of those things you are trying to do before the babies come? You are doing them while building those babies. Why can you not see how much you are accomplishing? I can't help you with the pregnancy, so why can't you let me help you with the rest? Hmm?"

Because it would make her love him even more.

And then what? He wouldn't leave. She knew that much. He wouldn't let her leave, either. Not again. Not ever.

It was oddly humbling to realize that.

She flipped the pillow away and looked at him. He had loosened his bow tie and opened a couple of shirt buttons, which only made his tuxedo look sexier.

"Do you feel stuck with me?" she asked, confronting the root question.

"No." He looked affronted she would ask. "I feel privileged that I'm starting a family with someone I respect and admire. You are the one who is stuck, *chérie*. You will always be the mother of Sauveterre twins. My mother can tell you that comes with serious drawbacks." He reached higher to set his hand on the side of her belly. "*I* have placed a burden on *you*. At least let me carry what I can of it."

She considered that as she looked into his hazel-green eyes. She loved him *so much*. What was the point in keeping hostility between them when they would be together for the rest of their lives? Holding him at arm's length certainly wasn't the way to win his heart. Letting him see how much she cared might.

"Can I sleep in your bed tonight?"

Something flashed in his gaze and his body tensed. "I won't let you leave it," he warned.

Oddly, as monumental and terrifying as his implacable possessiveness was, it also reassured her that they were a unit, moving into the future *together*.

"I know," she whispered.

He rose in a fluid motion, drawing her up with him, then letting her lead him to the room he was using.

He closed the door and turned on the light.

"Don't!" She shot out an anxious hand.

He released a ragged laugh and pulled at his clothes so roughly she could hear how little care he was taking.

Despite the near blackness, she moved to the blinds and gave them an extra twist then tugged the drapes fully closed.

"You really think the dark offers you any sort of protection, *chérie*?"

He was suddenly behind her, naked. She started at the touch of his hands, not because she hadn't heard him coming, but at the zing of electricity he sent through her.

He gathered her hair out of the way and found the zipper on her dress.

As it loosened, she turned in his arms and put hers around his neck, offering her mouth to his hot, hungry kiss. She moaned, closing her eyes in the darkness, but feeling dampness against her lashes as emotion welled. She kissed him back, hard.

"You missed this, too." He slid the fabric away and pressed his lips to her neck. "But don't be frantic. We have a lifetime now. I'll take care of you, but *gently*."

She wanted to protest and tell him to go fast, but he kissed her again, languorously, smoothly skimming her dress away, then taking his time tracing the lace across her hips, slowly, slowly working it down her thighs.

She panted as she waited for it to fall away, to be bare to his touch.

He turned her and leaned to set light kisses across her upper chest, skin brushing skin in a whisper. His hand drifted to pet her mound.

"Yes. Please." She covered his hand.

"Shh. I'll make it good, I promise." He explored deeper, carefully.

She caught her breath and arched into his touch, reaching to hold on to him as she let him take control of her pleasure.

"*Oui, chérie*, you love this, don't you? I do, too."

The closest he'd ever come to telling her he loved her and she could only gasp, digging fingernails behind his neck as she responded to his touch with a rock of her hips.

"That feels so good." She rubbed her face into the spicy aftershave in his throat, purring like a cat enjoying strokes.

How had she resisted this for all these weeks? *Why?*

His free hand moved over her, shaping her hip, cupping her bottom, encouraging her to move against the hand still nestled between her thighs.

They shifted hot skin against one another, trying to get closer, angling this way and that, finding each other's lips and kissing. Kissing and kissing for eternity.

"You're so hot." She slid her hand down his front, finding where he was pulled taut with arousal and clasping him, remembering all the ways to make him groan and push into her touch.

"Say it," he commanded her. "Tell me exactly what you want, *chérie*. I won't have accusations in the morning."

"I want you inside me, Henri. This." She caressed his smooth, hard shape and ran her thumb into the point beneath the tip, feeling him pulse in her palm. *"Please."*

He pressed a groan of abject hunger into her neck, opened his mouth to suck a love bite there. The sting caused a delicious counterpoint to the sweet pleasure of his touch parting her wet folds. She clenched on his fingers and cried out, holding tight to him as climax flooded through her in a rush, so powerful her knees folded.

He held her up, one hard arm around her back, releasing a jagged laugh of triumph against her skin, soothing, caressing, keeping her pulses going and maintaining her arousal.

"Nothing excites me more than knowing I do that to you," he told her, backing her toward the bed. "Nothing makes me want you more. I want to eat you alive. Have you in a thousand ways. Tie us both to this bed and never leave it."

He pressed her onto her back at the edge, leaning on one hand, looming over her as he guided himself against her, rubbing and nudging where she was plump and slippery and welcoming. Still tingling.

"Don't tease," she protested.

"Want?"

"So much."

"How much?" He gave her just the tip.

"More." She used her heel in his buttock to urge him deeper, releasing an unfettered groan as he sank into her.

For a moment there was nothing except the pleasure of returning to this place of joy. Ecstasy.

He said, "Cinnia," like he was exactly as overcome. Then, after a long time, he said, "I don't want to hurt you. Tell me if it's too deep." He caught under her legs and offered a few shallow strokes. His whole body was trembling with strain.

"Show me you want me, Henri."

"How can you doubt it?" he growled. "I'm so hard I hurt." He moved with deliberation, carefully withdrew then pressed as deeply as he could. Tingling sensations pushed into her, so sharp they were almost too much to bear.

"There," she cried as she lifted her hips to meet his and he folded over her. They melded together, mouths, bodies, kissing deeply with abandon. Then she slapped her hands far out to her sides and nudged her hips up against his, urging him to move with more purpose. "Take me."

He ground out a few muttered imprecations, trying to hold a civilized pace, but they were on a plateau of acute, mutual pleasure. Each stroke was a delicate torture that kept her on exactly the knife's edge of wanting orgasm, but withholding it.

She caught at his shoulders and dragged her nails down his arms. "You're not going to break me," she said fiercely. "*Do* it. Harder. Faster."

"You are going to break *me*." He thrust with more power. "Stop me if—"

"Yes!" she cried. "Like that!" She moved with him, meeting his thrusts, keening under the onslaught of pleasure. And there it was. Culmination. Hovering before her, detonating around them.

"Now, Henri. Please… With me," she gasped, shuddering with climax.

He abandoned his grip on his restraint, and let out a

shout of gratification, holding himself deep inside her as they both shattered with rapture.

It was beautiful and perfect and she smiled as he shifted them into the bed and settled her to fall asleep in his arms.

But just as she began to drift, her smile faded. She opened her eyes to the dark. He hadn't answered her question. In fact, as her pregnancy continued to take a toll and she leaned on him more and more, the answer became obvious.

Henri didn't *need* her for one single thing.

CHAPTER NINE

CINNIA WAS ENTERING her thirty-first week, feeling big as a house, but healthy enough that her doctor agreed she could travel to Spain for a few days. Angelique and Kasim were hosting a very small, private engagement party of immediate relatives in the Sauveterre compound. The formal announcement wouldn't be made for a few more months, due to Kasim's situation in Zhamair, but they were eager for their siblings to get to know one another.

The gathering was relaxing and lovely, giving Cinnia something she had longed for the first time with Henri: a sense of being a real part of his family. She and Trella had grown closer since their pregnancies, and Angelique had always been warm and welcoming. Now the twins felt like real sisters, calling her into their rooms to try on this draped top or one-size skirt, sharing little confidences along with a sample of hand cream or asking an opinion on a color of lipstick. His mother trimmed her hair when Cinnia bemoaned that going to the stylist was too much trouble when it was such a horrid crush of cameras.

Then there was Hasna, Sadiq's new wife and Kasim's sister.

Angelique had met Kasim when she and Trella had been designing Hasna's wedding gown. Cinnia already knew Sadiq. He was the most trusted friend Henri and Ramon had. She had actually been invited to the wedding in Zhamair, but she and Henri had broken up right before it.

Hasna made her feel like an integral part of the inner circle when she told her in private that Sadiq was very happy to see her again. "He was *so* upset when he heard that you and Henri had split. It bothered him for weeks."

"Sadiq and Hasna seem really happy," Cinnia said to Henri later, as they were preparing for bed. "I've missed him."

"Me, too," Henri said drily. "This is the first time I've seen him since the wedding. But yes, they do seem happy. I'm pleased for him."

"I don't think I've ever asked how he became such a fixture in your lives. I mean he's not—" She took off her earrings, recalling how often Henri had switched plans to accommodate his friend coming into town or making a point of catching up with him if they had an opportunity. "I'm trying to figure out how to say this nicely. He's not like most of the people I've met through you. He always came out to Ramon's races, but he didn't care about cars. I guess you do business together, but he seems more passionate about computers and software. I'm trying to figure out what you and Ramon have in common with him."

Sadiq was soft-spoken and quick to laugh, but didn't make jokes or put forth strong opinions. He was the male version of a wallflower when he was around the Sauveterre men.

"I see so many people trying to *gain* your attention," she pointed out. "He isn't like that at all. Which answers my question about why you like him, but I'm still wondering how you ever got to know him well enough in the first place, to know that he would make such a good friend."

Henri was silent as he removed his shirt and unbuckled his pants.

"We met at school." He stripped to his snug navy blue underwear. "The day Trella was taken." He folded his pants on a hanger and placed them on the rung. "He was on the steps next to Ramon. Saw it happen and ran in to find me."

"Oh." She was already in her nightgown and paused in pulling back the sheets. "I had no idea."

"I don't talk about it," he said flatly. "But he was instrumental in our locating her. He *is* passionate about his computers and was able to help the police by hacking into the math tutor's computer. Afterward, he was one of the few men Trella could tolerate being around other than family. Maybe because he saved her, maybe because his personality is, as you say, low-key. Either way, we didn't care. He was a hero in our eyes and has always been a true friend."

He turned off the closet light and moved into the bathroom to brush his teeth.

Cinnia crawled into bed, stunned by Henri being so open, but thinking, *be careful what you wish for.* It was so disturbing. She hurt terribly for him.

But she was oddly encouraged that he'd chosen to share this with her. Their relationship wasn't perfect, but she was back to believing he cared for her to some degree. Perhaps he was coming to entrust her with his heart if he was willing to entrust her with his most painful memory.

When he came to bed a few minutes later, she snuggled close, wanting to offer comfort even though he was stiff and unreceptive.

"I didn't mean to bring up bad memories," she said, fitting herself under his arm and kissing his shoulder. "Every time I think of it, I wish that I could take away how scared you must have been."

"I wasn't scared, I was *guilty*," Henri acknowledged in a soft hiss.

Cinnia drew back a fraction, trying to see him in the filtered light. "How?" She knew the whole family had had therapy at different times in their efforts to heal from the incident. He must know he wasn't at fault. "You were fifteen. Victims are never to blame for the hurt done to them."

"I was talking to a girl."

His tone reminded her of the day he'd let his hatred of the press burst out of him, like he had kept it pent up too long. There was also a quality of confessing the worst crime in history, as if he'd never told anyone what he was saying to her now.

"Trella came by and said she was going outside. I told her to *go*. I wanted privacy, but Trella was *my* responsibility. That's how it always was with the four of us. Ramon kept an eye on Gili, I watched out for Bella. I might as well have handed her to them."

Her heart stalled. This poor man.

"Henri, if you had been outside to stop Trella, they would have gone for Angelique," she argued, lifting on an elbow. "That's not a better outcome."

"If they'd called out to Angelique, she would have made Ramon go with her. She was shy. We might as well have had a fighting chance at stopping it before it happened. I should have told Trella to wait for me, but I didn't." He pinched the bridge of his nose.

"Because you were talking to a girl."

She was trying to make him see how insignificant that was, but a chill moved into her heart. A realization was dawning, but it was a dark one. More like a shadow dimming the landscape inside her.

"Who was she?" Her ears rang, making it nearly impossible to hear his response.

"Just a girl."

Cinnia pulled all the way back onto her own pillow, no longer touching him. She wanted to ease his conscience, she really did, but said, "No, she wasn't." She didn't know how she knew it, she just did. "There were lots of girls after that. She wasn't *just* a girl."

"I don't want to talk about this. Go to sleep."

"You cared about her," she said in realization. It hurt. Oh, it hurt like acid and corrosive and nuclear waste, all being poured over her heart.

"*Mon Dieu.* It was puppy love, Cinnia. You had that yourself and know it means nothing."

"No, it doesn't. Not when it means… This is why you won't let yourself care for me. You're worried it will impact your ability to take care of the rest of your family."

"I *care* for you, damn it."

"But you don't *love* me. You're never going to love me, are you? You will never let yourself feel anything like it because you think it takes too much of your attention. Do you know how hard this is, Henri?" She gave the mattress a smack with her fist. "I've fought and fought falling in love with you. I've let myself rely on you. I sleep with you and I'm having children with you. And you can't even love me back? You won't even *try*."

"You love me?" He rolled toward her.

"Yes, and I'm *sorry*. I know it's one more burden you don't want!"

"That's not true." He reached for her.

"I keep telling myself to give you time, that you'll come around, but you are never going to relent, are you? It's not because I'm not lovable. You're just that stubborn!"

"Cinnia." He tried to gather her into his front.

"No." She rolled so her back was toward him. "I want to go to sleep."

"Cin," he cajoled, pressing his lips to her shoulder as he fit himself behind her.

"Don't touch me." She pushed at his leg with her foot and brushed his hand off her hip. "It's one thing to put something in a cage because you love it and want to protect it, but when you don't actually care, it just makes me a prisoner. So forget it. No conjugal visit."

"Stop it. You're blowing this out of proportion." His hand settled on her waist.

"I'm *tired*." Her voice broke. She was *so* tired of wishing and yearning and winding up empty. She pushed his hand off her, wriggling so she was on the very edge of the bed. "Leave me alone."

He swore and threw off the covers, leaving the bed and their room.

Cinnia woke late, alone, eyes like sandpaper. She held a cold compress on them, somehow pulled herself together with a comb and a toothbrush, put on a sundress that wasn't too much like a circus tent and went downstairs, raw as an exposed nerve.

Everyone was outside, seeming in good spirits, which made her depression all the harder to disguise. She pretended she was merely tired when she joined Hasna at the table under the umbrella. Trella was on a nearby lounger, showing something to her mother on her tablet. Kasim and Sadiq stood with Angelique at the rail, laying bets on the tennis match below.

Henri and Ramon were on the court, trying to kill one another. She'd seen them play before and they were hideously competitive, equally strong and skilled, and they knew each other's weaknesses. Their games could go on for ages.

"They're so well matched," Hasna said, craning her

neck. "I suppose loyalty demands you put your money on Henri."

In the mood he was in, yes, he would likely prevail. In the mood she was in? She'd love to see him lose abysmally, especially to Ramon. That always annoyed the hell out of him.

"Is this the yogurt we heard so much about yesterday?" Cinnia looked over the tubs set in ice. "They got away okay this morning?" she asked of the guests who'd brought it.

"They did and, yes, it is," Hasna said with an absent smile. "Ooh, that's tied it up again. Goodness, this is a nail-biter. The muesli is very good, too," she added over her shoulder, then looked back to the rapid *plonk, plonk* of the ball.

Cinnia avoided the pink-tinged yogurt and went for the plain, sprinkling muesli without really looking and reseated herself to take a bite. She started to ask Trella what she was reading and felt the first tingle streak from the roof of her mouth down the back of her throat.

She swore. "The muesli." She grabbed Hasna's wrist. "Does it have dried strawberries? Call an ambulance." Her tongue felt like it was swelling as she spoke. "Call Henri. Tell him I need my pen."

"What?" Hasna asked with incomprehension.

"I'm allergic." Her throat was growing raspy. She watched Hasna's fear turning to pain as Cinnia increased her grip, driven by terror to impress how bad this was. She was barely able to force out the rest of her words. "To strawberries."

"Henri!" Hasna screamed at the top of her lungs, standing to wave at him. "Cinnia ate a strawberry!"

Distantly she heard Trella say something, maybe that she would call an ambulance. Cinnia wasn't tracking, just closed her eyes and gripped the edge of the table, concentrating on breathing, managing long, slow, strained wheezes. Rapid footsteps ran toward her and hard hands grasped her, moving her to a lounger. She kept her eyes closed, feeling like she was sipping tiny drinks of air through a narrow straw. A tiny, hollow piece of dry grass. Her throat strained, trying to pull her breaths through the constriction.

Henri's voice was hard as he shouted for her purse. She opened her eyes. He looked gray. Angry.

Scared.

There was a spare pen behind the mirror in their bathroom. Did he remember that? She wanted to reach out to him, grab him, but her limbs felt heavy and her hands were on fire. Her ears itched inside her head and her brain had gone swimming.

A sting went into her thigh, like a bite or the snap of a rubber band.

"That's one," Henri said, cupping the side of her face very forcefully. "Stay with me, *chérie*. Breathe."

She tried. *The babies*, she tried to say, but her lips were fat and numb. Tears filled her eyes. She was scared. Her entire body felt as though it was glowing with fire, her skin cooking, too tight to contain all this heat. What if her carelessness hurt the twins?

Henri took his hand away from her cheek as he accepted something. Another stab went into her thigh and he rubbed it hard.

She closed her eyes, begging the medicine to work, trying to listen for the ambulance, but her heart was pounding so loud she couldn't hear anything. It took everything in her to draw a breath, then to focus on pulling in one more.

Her hand hurt. Henri was holding it and his voice was *furious*. "Cinnia. *Breathe*."

She was *trying*.

* * *

Cinnia had been right last night, but he'd refused to admit it. He was being stubborn. He had shut her down. Shut her out.

But even as he had left her, fully aware she was beginning to cry, he had told himself this was for her own good. He was keeping her *safe* by keeping a clear head and withholding his heart.

Her safety meant everything.

Then he'd heard Hasna scream, *"Cinnia ate a strawberry!"*

He added it to the list of worst phrases he'd ever heard.

"We're here." Ramon appeared at his side and clamped a hard arm across his shoulders.

Henri staggered, only then realizing he was swaying on his feet.

On his other side, Trella took his arm. "Where is she? What did they say?"

Henri realized he was standing in the middle of the hospital hallway, staring at the doors where Cinnia had been whisked away from him. Of course Ramon was here on the heels of the ambulance. Of course their pregnant sister had climbed into the passenger seat for that hair-raising ride.

"Her blood pressure dropped," Henri said, repeating all the terrible, terrible words. They detonated fresh explosions of despair as they left his lips and hit on fresh ears. "They said the babies might not be getting enough oxygen. They're taking them."

"Taking—" Trella gasped. Ramon swore.

"I should call her mother," Henri said, dreading it. He had failed. *I'm so sorry.*

He didn't think he could manage it.

"Mama is calling her. Kasim said he would arrange a flight to bring her." Trella pulled out her phone while

Ramon physically helped Henri to sit. "I'll relay that she's gone into surgery. Was she conscious in the ambulance? They gave her something, right? Medicine? She was breathing? She'll be okay?"

"She was trying," Henri said, throat raw from shouting at her, as if that would help. "They put a tube in her throat. Then she had a seizure. She wasn't conscious after that."

Ramon was crushing him with that hard arm across his shoulders, but Henri crumpled forward, elbows on his knees, stomach churning. Putting his hands over his eyes didn't help. He still saw her blue lips, still felt the strength go out of her grip.

"Oh, Henri." He could hear the plea for reassurance in his sister's voice, but he had none to offer. He was terrified.

"I saw the yogurt this morning. I saw it had strawberries and I made a mental note she shouldn't have any." He had been restless, hadn't slept properly. He'd been feeling guilty and angry and small. Defensive.

When Ramon had asked if he wanted to play tennis, he'd let the activity consume him, working out his frustrations in a hail of powerful volleys.

"I shouldn't have been playing tennis. I should have been there, at the table, waiting for her, ready to warn her."

"We all knew she was allergic. You told us last year when she came for your birthday. We just weren't thinking," Trella soothed. "Cinnia is always careful, too. She always asks. I don't know why she didn't today."

"We'd had a fight. She wasn't thinking."

"This is not your fault, Henri." Trella's small hand dug into his arm, trying to press the words into him.

It *was* his fault.

If he had said the words that Cinnia had asked for last night, the ones that had burst out of him in the ambulance, everything would be different right now.

I know it's one more burden you don't want...

She loved him. He'd been touched, elated, filled with such tenderness he had reached to gather her in, wanting to hold her against his heart.

Then she had said something about feeling like a prisoner and kicked him out of bed.

He had walked out on a sense of righteousness, telling himself he would not let her make him feel obligated, but when had Cinnia ever done that to him? She had begun to lean on him lately, literally holding his arm out of physical exhaustion, but she had been carrying her love for him like a dogged little soldier, refusing to *burden* him with it.

He had always expected to feel hampered by love, but *Cinnia's* love? Her sunny smiles and cheeky asides, her passion and even that streak of pigheadedness had kept him going for two years, not that he'd realized it at the time. It was only as he looked back on their separation, recalled how short-tempered he'd been after Cinnia had left, picking fights with Gili, of all people, that he recognized how badly he'd been missing Cinnia.

Since she'd been back with him, it had been one adjustment after another, but he'd attacked all of the changes with determined energy, eager to carve out her permanent place in his life. He hadn't just accommodated her. He'd made her part of his foundation. He wanted to *marry* her.

Because he couldn't live without her. There was no point.

Why hadn't he told her all of that last night?

"I tried to tell her I loved her. In the ambulance. I don't think she heard me."

"She knows," Trella said, brushing the tickling wetness from his cheek. "She knows, Henri. I promise you."

"No. She doesn't." Because he had refused to say it. Refused to admit it even to himself until it was too late. "I do all these things, go to such great lengths, to try to keep us all safe. I told her she could trust me and what happens? *A goddamned strawberry.* What am I going to do if I lose her? What if I lose all of them?"

CHAPTER TEN

CINNIA OPENED HER eyes to such bright light, she immediately shut them again. Where was she? She peeked again at the tiled ceiling, the stainless-steel contraption beside her with an IV bag hanging off it.

Hospital?

Oh, right. She winced and tried to touch her belly, apprehensive because it didn't feel nearly so heavy as it should.

Someone had hold of her hand.

"Chérie." Henri's whisper had grit in it. He carried the back of her hand to his closed mouth as he stood to loom over her.

She peered from one eye. He looked gorgeous even when he looked horrible. His eyes were sunk into dark sockets, his jaw coated in stubble, his clothes wrinkled.

Her eyes welled with fear.

She tried to say *the babies?* but her throat was a desert that caught fire as she tried to speak.

"Les filles sont très bien. Our daughters are beautiful," Henri said with quiet urgency, setting his hand on the side of her face. "They're very small, but they're little fighters." He stroked her cheek. "Just like their mama. And so alike, Cinnia." He gave his head a bemused shake. "They are the most magical thing I have ever seen."

She started to smile, but her mouth trembled with emotion. "Can I—" She cut herself off with a wince and a moan, touching her throat. Talking really hurt, but she glanced toward the door. She wanted to see them. *Bring them to me.*

"You had a tube in your throat. That's why it hurts." He leaned to press the call button. "The nurse was just in here, said your vitals are good, but the doctor will want to come now you're awake. I'll get the girls."

First he lowered to set his mouth on her forehead, holding the kiss for a long moment, slowly drawing back with such a look in his eyes it made her throat ache in a different way.

"Do not ever do that to me again. Not ever," he said gravely.

"Deliver twins?" she joked in a dry whisper.

"Not funny." His eyes winced shut, lashes appearing matted with wetness when he opened them. They were practically nose to nose. The emotion in his eyes made her catch her breath. He stroked the backs of his fingers against her cheek and started to say something.

The nurse bustled in, forcing him to straighten in a jerk and cast a scowl at the poor woman.

Minutes later, Cinnia met her daughters, tearing up all over again as Henri and a nurse set their tiny swaddled forms into her shaking arms.

"You're sure they're okay?" She wanted to squish them tight, but held them like fragile eggshells. She couldn't take her eyes off their identical little faces with their rosebud mouths and button noses, one sleeping soundly, the other blinking blue eyes at her.

"Colette needed a little oxygen at first and they're both still working on regulating their body temperatures, but they're taking a bottle and squawking when they want more." Henri's hand looked ridiculously huge, overwhelming the tiny form as he splayed his fingers ever so gently on the infant in her right arm.

"Colette?" That was not a name she had had on her mental list, but it suited the inquisitive gaze that met hers.

"And Rosalina," he said with a rueful smile, moving to use one fingertip to adjust the edge of the blanket away from Rosalina's cheek. "We are under no obligation to keep those names, but my sisters refused to call them Twin One and Twin Two. Given the custody battle going on in the nursery between them and the grandmothers, we'll be lucky to have our *own* names on the birth certificates."

"They're perfect. *Hola*, Rosalina. *Bonjour*, Colette," she whispered, pressing a kiss to each girl's warm, soft forehead. "Wait. Grandmothers? Mum is here?"

"*Oui.* And she's as anxious to see you as you were to see *your* daughters. Let's let the doctor do his thing so we can reassure her you're recovering."

Cinnia allowed the babies to be whisked back to the nursery and thirty minutes of playing snakes and ladders with her dignity followed. She suffered exams and questions and prodding. On the plus side, she was allowed a drink of water, a facecloth, a hairbrush and, best of all, a *toothbrush*.

She learned they were well into the afternoon of the day *after* she had taken her near-fatal taste of strawberry-tainted muesli.

"I'm going to devote my life to eradicating that particular fruit from the planet," Henri muttered as the doctor finished up his own riot act about the dangers of anaphylactic shock while pregnant.

"I'm *sorry*," Cinnia said, wincing at the trouble she'd caused.

The doctor pronounced her well enough to be wheeled down the hall to try nursing the twins and the nurse left to fetch a chair.

As they were left alone, Henri hitched his hip on the bed beside her. At least she was sitting up now, beginning to feel human again.

"I am sorry," she said with genuine remorse, unnerved by the way he looked at her with such deep emotion in his eyes. It made her feel compressed. Breathless. "I saw the pink yogurt and thought the plain would be fine. I didn't even look properly at the muesli."

"*I* am sorry, *chérie*," Henri took her hand and handled it very gently, turning it over as though examining it. "I keep expecting to see bruises. Your bones could have broken, I was holding on to you so tightly. I was so afraid it wouldn't be tight enough."

"Mum is going to ground me for sure," she said, trying to make light because his shaken tone made her insides tremble. "Has anyone told my sisters? They won't let me hear the end of it."

"Ramon is at the airport, collecting them."

"Oh, no, seriously? I'm *so* sorry."

"I'm not trying to make you feel guilty. I'm telling you we were worried. We all love you very much. We didn't want to lose you."

Her heart caught and she tried to pull her hand from his.

He made a noise of refusal and held on. "You didn't hear me in the ambulance. I *love* you, Cinnia."

"You don't have to say that just because—"

"I *do* need to say it. I should have said it when you asked back in January. Before that even." He scowled in self-re-crimination. "Hospitals are excellent places for confronting your failings. Cowardice. Wrongful thinking. Time wasted that could have been spent with someone who brings joy into your life. I can spell out all my mistakes, but I don't have to because you know all of them. You know *me*. You say I'm a closed book, but you know me, Cinnia. In ways no one else does."

He pressed her hand to his thigh, looked into her eyes with so much openness it was like standing over the Grand Canyon, her mind incapable of taking in the vastness before her.

"I took you for granted. I expected you to just *be* there," he continued. "But that *is* all I need from you, *mon amour*. I know you want to help me pay the bills or make my dental appointments. You want to play a role so you feel you are pulling your weight, but what I need most from you is *you*. I need you to *be* with me. *Alive*."

The corners of her mouth pulled, lips trembling, chastised, but deeply touched. "It's hard to feel like I'm enough," she confessed, stroking his thigh. "When you're...you."

"Who else can I trust with my heart? Hmm?" He cupped the side of her face. "I didn't ask you to carry it, but you picked it up and took such care with it all this time."

She had, and all the while she had felt like it was turned away from her. Now, suddenly, love was shining back at her, gleaming from his eyes and his heart and his soul, bathing her in a light so blinding her eyes watered.

"I want yours, *chérie*," he said tenderly. "Will you give it to me?"

Her throat closed and her chest felt tight. "It's always been yours."

He shifted, rising to stand, then set his knee on the mattress beside her hip. "You told me to get down on one knee, but I'll be damned if I'll do that on a hospital floor."

She caught back a laugh even as she caught her breath.

"I mean this, *chérie*."

She knew what was coming, but was still unprepared. "I love you, Cinnia. Will you marry me?"

The words expanded the air around them so everything disappeared except this beautiful man holding her hand, holding her gaze. Her heart grew so big, pounded so hard, she thought it would burst with happiness. Her eyes flooded and such love filled her, she could only lift her arms and say, "Yes. Of course. I love you. Yes."

He gathered her close and they kissed, first briefly, tenderly, then with deeper feeling. Passion, but something else that was healing and unifying, solemn and binding.

"Enough of that," the nurse said as she interrupted. "The babies you've already made are still fresh. And hungry, Mama. Let's take you to them."

Henri wheeled her, impulsively kissing the top of her hair as they went into the warm nursery. Her mother was cradling a sleeping Rosalina while Elisa Sauveterre was fending off her daughters from Colette, who was fussing and rooting with hunger.

"Oh, love," Milly said, letting Henri take Rosalina so she could hug Cinnia. "This is the last time you do this, do you hear me?"

"Get engaged?" Cinnia teased, sending a cheeky wink to Henri. "Agreed."

The women erupted in excitement, kissing and congratulating Henri.

"Have you set a date?" Angelique demanded, clasping her hands with excitement. "Have a double ceremony with me and Kasim!"

"I don't want to wait that long." Henri was still holding Rosalina, but he grazed the backs of his fingers against Cinnia's cheek in a tender caress. "We can wait until you're discharged if we have to, but right after. *Oui?*"

"Why wait until I'm discharged?" Cinnia held his gaze

in a small dare. "What do you think, Mum? Could you arrange something for tomorrow? Since everyone is here?"

"What?"

"Are you serious?" A smile grew on Henri's lips.

"Are you?"

"Never more." There wasn't a shred of hesitation in his expression. "I love you with everything in me. I can't wait to call you my wife."

"Then yes, let's do it." She lifted her lips for a quick, sweet kiss, then gave her attention to the women. "Ladies, your assignment, if you choose to accept it, is to plan a wedding for tomorrow."

"Way to clear a room," Henri said drily a moment later, as she latched the hungry Colette.

"Do you want something more formal?" she asked with sudden concern. "A longer engagement?"

"Hell, no. Once you see what's going on outside these walls, you won't want anything to do with being a Sauveterre. No, I am perfectly happy to keep the wedding small and fast and do it while we have a semblance of privacy."

For a ceremony thrown together at the last minute in the hospital chapel, it was touching and beautiful. Cinnia wore an ivory sundress altered by the twin designers into an elegant afternoon wedding creation. Her sister Priscilla brought all her modeling skills to bear as she did Cinnia's makeup and hair. Nell handled the music, the grandmothers took care of the bouquet and flowers, Ramon stood up for Henri and Dorry witnessed for Cinnia.

The rings were tied to ribbons around their swaddled daughters, who were held tenderly by the aunties who had named them. Fortunately the aisle was short since Cinnia could only manage a few steps.

Her husband put a possessive, bolstering arm around her

as she arrived next to him. He was rested, clean shaven, wore a tailored gray suit and had a fresh haircut. The pride and contentment in his expression as he gazed down on her made her tuck her face into his shoulder, too moved to withstand how much she loved him.

But as they spoke their vows and exchanged their rings, she knew he loved her just as much. In this, the most important way, they were equal.

EPILOGUE

Four years later...

CINNIA MADE THE mistake of thinking that if the girls weren't with her, she could walk the few blocks from the clinic to her mother's flat without being noticed.

It was a nice day. She was wearing a sun hat and sunglasses. She was in a good mood and wanted to feel the early summer sun beaming down on her. The city wasn't yet overrun with tourists. Surely she could get away with it?

Not.

A Swedish couple noticed her and the selfies started. Her guards helped her navigate the handful of pedestrians who then accosted her. Everyone was very polite, but very quickly there were too many of them. She skipped with a sigh of relief into the quiet of the lobby, where she waved at the doorman and headed to the lift.

Henri was waiting for her when she entered. "I thought you'd be here ahead of me."

"I walked. Big mistake. Now the paparazzi will be waiting when we leave. Sorry."

"Such a scandal, to be caught meeting my wife for an afternoon tryst in her mother's empty apartment," he said, scooping her into his arms and kissing her with enough enthusiasm to make her heart race as quickly as it had the first time he'd kissed her. He drew back. "How was the appointment?"

"We can go." She smiled with anticipation. They occasionally managed a weekend away, leaving the girls with family, but most of their alone time was stolen here in an afternoon. Which was lovely, but with another baby coming, they'd decided to book a week on an island so long as she was cleared to travel.

"And?" he prompted.

"One." She set aside her sunglasses and handbag, then linked her arms around his neck. Her tennis bracelet slid down from her left wrist and her stylish and subtle, beautifully engraved, gold allergy bracelet skimmed down her right. It didn't do a thing to protect her really, except to remind her daily to be very careful what she ate, but Henri liked her to wear it, so she did.

"Are you disappointed?"

"Never." He closed one eye, considering. "But I think you will get an earful from other quarters."

"I know, right?" She wrinkled her nose in amusement.

Their daughters had recently reached an age of enough understanding to ask where Mama's twin was. Papa had a twin. *They* had a twin. Where was Mama's twin?

Cinnia had explained about singles and twins. They had cousins who were singles, remember? Not everyone had a twin.

Colette, being her father's daughter, had taken the explanation with equanimity. She had snuggled into Cinnia's lap with a despondent little sigh and said, "That's sad." A hug and a kiss later, she'd been off to other more important things, like learning to write her name.

Rosy had been beside herself. That was *not* right, she insisted crossly. Mama *must* have a twin. Where was she? *Go get her.* She had cried on and off for days.

"Merci, chérie."

"For?" she asked, smiling up at him.

"Our children. The joy you give me, every day."

"We're not even in bed yet." She nudged her hips into his, feeling him harden against her as she gave him a smoky look. "Take me there. I'll show you joy."

"I *love* your libido when you're pregnant. Do you know that? I love *you*." He backed her toward the wall.

"Ooh. Look who's feeling sentimental. Shall we open the windows? Have you arranged fireworks?"

"You deliver joy, I deliver fireworks," he vowed, catching at her mouth with a brief kiss. "I think about our first time often. Don't you? It's one of my favorite memories."

"It *was* a good night," she acknowledged.

"It was very good. Let me remind you *how* good."

Lucky her, he had an excellent talent for recall.

* * * * *

If you enjoyed
HIS MISTRESS WITH TWO SECRETS,
don't forget to read the first instalment of
THE SAUVETERRE SIBLINGS *quartet*
PURSUED BY THE DESERT PRINCE
Available now!

And why not explore these other
great Dani Collins reads?
THE SECRET BENEATH THE VEIL
BOUGHT BY HER ITALIAN BOSS
THE MARRIAGE HE MUST KEEP
THE CONSEQUENCE HE MUST CLAIM
Available now!

MILLS & BOON®

MODERN™

POWER, PASSION AND IRRESISTIBLE TEMPTATION

MILLS & BOON®

EXCLUSIVE EXTRACT

Persuading plain Jane to marry him was easy
enough – but Shiekh Zayed Al Zawba hadn't
bargained on the irresistible curves hidden under
her clothes, or that she is deliciously untouched.
When Jane begins to tempt him beyond his
wildest dreams, leaving their marriage
unconsummated becomes impossible…

Read on for a sneak preview of
THE SHEIKH'S BOUGHT WIFE

It was difficult to be *distant* when your body seemed to
have developed a stubborn will of its own. When she found
herself wanting to push her aching breasts against Zayed's
powerful chest as he caught her in his arms for the traditional first dance between bride and groom. As it was, she
could barely think straight and wasn't it the most infuriating
thing in the world that he immediately seemed to pick up
on that?

'You seem to be having trouble breathing, dear wife,'
he murmured as he moved her to the center of the marble
dance floor.

'The dress is very tight.'

'I'd noticed.' He twirled her around, holding her back
a little. 'It looks very well on you.'

She forced a tight smile but she didn't relax. 'Thank you.'

'Or maybe it is the excitement of having me this close
to you which is making you pant like a little kitten?'

'You're *annoying* me, rather than exciting me. And I do
wish you'd stop trying to get underneath my skin.'

'Don't you like people getting underneath your skin, Jane?'

'No,' she said honestly. 'I don't.'

'Why not?'

She met the blaze of his ebony eyes and suppressed a shiver. 'Does everything have to have a reason?'

'In my experience, yes.' There was a pause. 'Has a man hurt you in the past?'

This was her chance to tell him yes—even though the very idea that someone had got that close to her was laughable.

Zayed had already guessed she might be a virgin, but that didn't even come close to her shameful lack of experience.

Trying to ignore the way his groin was brushing against her as he edged her closer, she glanced up at him, her cheeks burning. 'I refuse to answer that on the grounds that I might incriminate myself. Tell me instead, do you always insist on interrogating women when you're dancing with them?'

'No. I don't,' he said simply. 'But then I've never had a bride before and I've never danced with a woman who was so determined not to give anything of herself away.'

'And that's the only reason you want to know,' she said quietly. 'Because you like a challenge.'

'All men like a challenge, Jane.' His black eyes gleamed. 'Haven't you learned that by now?'

She didn't answer—because how was she qualified to answer any questions about what men did or didn't like?

Don't miss
THE SHEIKH'S BOUGHT WIFE
By Sharon Kendrick

Available May 2017
www.millsandboon.co.uk